FIRST TIMES

Edited by

Robert Dunbar

POOLBEG

Published 1997
by Poolbeg Press Ltd
123 Baldoyle Industrial Estate
Dublin 13, Ireland

The Publishers gratefully acknowledge the support of The Arts Council.

A catalogue record for this book is available from the British Library.

ISBN 1 85371 762 2

Cover design by Poolbeg Group Services Ltd
Set by Poolbeg Group Services Ltd in Times 11/13
Printed by The Guernsey Press Ltd,
Vale, Guernsey, Channel Islands.

CONTENTS

BACKYARD MAJESTY
Mary Arrigan   1

SPOTS
Mary Beckett   12

UNEVEN GROUND
Michael Carroll   19

THE OLD DOG
Marita Conlon-McKenna   26

THE VISIT
June Considine   32

THE NIGHT I FELT THE EARTH MOVE
Margrit Cruickshank   45

TAKING PICTURES
Rose Doyle   55

I WANT TO HOLD YOUR HAND
Soinbhe Lally   65

HONORARY MEMBER
Chris Lynch   77

BLIND CHANCE
Sam McBratney   89

A TIGHT TEAM
Gretta Mulrooney   99

SUMMER LOVE
Joan O'Neill   109

DAMSON JAM
Siobhán Parkinson   122

FIRST MEAT
Tom Richards   131

NO ONE UNDERSTANDS
Marilyn Taylor   142

ABOUT THE AUTHORS   153

ABOUT THE EDITOR   156

*"The distance is nothing; it is only
the first step that is difficult."*
Marquise Du Deffand

This anthology is dedicated – with happiest memories – to all my former students at Coleraine Technical College (1961-1966) and Rainey Endowed School, Magherafelt (1966-1980).

Robert Dunbar
Dublin, 1997

BACKYARD MAJESTY

Mary Arrigan

After we'd given back the suit that we borrowed for my confirmation, we examined the present that Miss Flanagan had given me.

"An old hen with four scrawny chicks is hardly a fitting gift for someone who lives in a street," Ma said, peering into the chest which housed the chirping brood.

"Ah, they'll be all right," volunteered Grandpa as he stroked one of the yellow chicks with his gnarled finger. "Sure won't they give us eggs later on. There's nothing as nice as eggs from hens that you're friendly with. Hens that see the sunlight and scratch the earth, not like those unfortunate creatures that are kept in cages and lay eggs on to conveyor belts. Zombies they are, that produce miserable eggs with no taste or colour."

Ma snorted and put the lid back on the tea chest. "With our luck they'll probably all turn out to be cocks. If we sell them now we'll get a few bob for them."

"No!" I protested. "They're mine. Miss Flanagan gave them to me."

"Well, you look after them," said Ma. "And if there's a hint of hen shit gets into the house, they're gone."

"We will," enthused Grandpa. "We'll look after them, Jim and me. Come on, lad." He lifted the chest and its protesting contents out into the yard. Our tiny back yard consisted of a small cobbled square with a turf shed, an outdoor lavatory and an ash-pit.

1

With a few yards of wire we rigged up a makeshift hen-run between the ash-pit and the shed and, by turning the tea-chest on its side and nailing some sacking over it, made an admirable hen house. We carved "1956" on to one of the wooden posts to remind us that our chicken farm started in my confirmation year.

With great pride Grandpa and I tended our livestock. We went to the library and borrowed books on the care and feeding of poultry. We dreamed of building up our stock and eventually having a huge poultry farm in the country with loads of people working for us.

"You're filling the lad's head with nonsense," muttered Ma.

"Just wait," Grandpa said patiently. "Just you wait until we're eating scrambled eggs fit for a king. And what harm is there in having dreams anyway? Isn't life drab enough? Now," he turned to me, "we'll need scraps. Plenty of scraps."

Thus, each day after school, I called on the neighbours who willingly scraped their leftovers into my new bucket. We watched our flock thrive, though I was sorry when the chicks lost their yellow fluff.

One evening Ma came home in a fury. We knew we were in trouble when we heard the door slam.

"Begging!" she stormed. Grandpa was frying sausages on the stove and I was setting the table. We looked up, startled. Ma threw her headscarf on the sofa. "Begging," she said again and dealt me a stinging blow on the ear. "Mrs Quinn asked me today if the hens were doing well on her scraps. I was never so embarrassed."

"Leave the chap alone," put in Grandpa, standing in front of me. "There's no harm in what he did. And, anyway, I put him up to it."

"Of course it was you," shouted Ma, shifting her venom to Grandpa. "What else do you put him up to when my back is turned?"

Ma's back was always turned. She worked long hours for little money in a pottery factory and came home in the evenings tired and irritable. To preserve her sanity, as she put it, she had what she called her "hope jug" on the dresser. Into this went any spare cash which might be left over at the end of the week. When a decent sum had accumulated, we'd take a trip on the train or a night at the pictures. But mostly the money would be used to pay some bill and we'd have to start over again. I often wished that the jug would suddenly get full and Ma would laugh and wear a nice dress.

One morning a letter came for Ma. Grandpa examined it closely, his bald head bent over it as he stood at the window.

"What class of a stamp is that?" he asked me. "I can't make it out."

"It's American," I said. I knew that because a friend had once let me see his stamp album in exchange for a dead frog.

"American, begob!" exclaimed Grandpa. "Who'd be writing to your mother from America?" He shook the letter and held it to the light and, when neither action revealed the contents, he stuck it behind the clock on the mantelpiece. All day he kept glancing at the envelope, wondering aloud about it.

"There's a letter for you," he shouted eagerly to Ma before she'd even closed the door. "From America."

She noted his childish curiosity and, trying to conceal her own excitement, said, "I'll read it later." Grandpa was defeated.

"Come on, lad," he poked me in the chest. "We'll feed our livestock."

Since I'd been banned from "begging", Grandpa picked up a bucket of scraps each day from the pub. They sometimes smelled of stale beer, but our fowl were fat and happy. Three of the chickens had grown into sturdy hens, but it was the cock that was our pride and joy. His tail rose in a graceful arc of blues and greens. His russet plumage glistened like polished mahogany brightening the drab little yard. Grandpa and I would spend ages leaning against the wire watching "Alfred the Great", as we called him, strutting with majestic superiority.

"Lord, but he's a beauty," Grandpa sighed with awe. "Look at the dignity of the fellow. He'd make a great fighter, given a pair of spurs and a good opponent." He laughed at my horrified face and ruffled my hair. The whole street had got to hear about Alfred and there was often a group of Grandpa's cronies gathered in admiration at the hen-house when I'd come in from school. My own pals bribed me with sweets and comics for glimpses of the famous fowl.

"This place is like a bloody zoo," said Ma. "Throw in a monkey and we could charge people."

On the day of the letter, she teased Grandpa's curiosity until after tea.

"We're having a visitor," she said finally, folding the damp tea-towel on a rail over the range.

"Who?" asked Grandpa.

"Uncle Joe," she replied, taking the letter from her pocket.

"Oh, him," scoffed Grandpa. "Is it him who wrote that letter? God, and there was me thinking it was from someone important."

Ma let the insult pass. She always spoke of Uncle Joe with the same tone of voice she used when speaking of our betters – people with full hope jugs. Uncle Joe was actually my grandmother's brother who'd gone to America years and years ago – I don't think my mother had ever even met him, but he was always held up by both herself and her mother as an example of someone who'd "got on". "Getting on" was an important phrase in Ma's vocabulary. She constantly hoped that, some day, she would rise above her present station – that there was something around the corner that would release us into a world of plenty.

"Old rip," Grandpa snorted between puffs on his pipe.

"He didn't even come to your mother's funeral. What does he want coming back now?"

"He wants to see the old home in Cork and to look up relatives."

"Humpf," said Grandpa. "The only relatives he'll find fly about on dark nights."

The next couple of weeks were spent in a flurry of preparation for the visiting uncle. Grandpa was scathing of the fuss.

"He's only an ordinary mortal like ourselves," he muttered, as he was made to clear out the old magazines and newspapers he'd accumulated under the cushions of his chair.

"He is not," snapped Ma. "He's got money and a big house. Not like certain members of the family." But Grandpa just laughed. "And for heaven's sake, put in your teeth," Ma hissed.

It was around this time that Alfred began to crow his full raucous cry in the mornings. Some of the neighbours complained.

"You'll get used to it," Grandpa told them. "Can you not think of anything nicer than being wakened by such a noble creature?"

The people on our street were early risers anyway since they mostly worked in Ma's factory or else in the furniture plant on the far side of town, so the complaints faded after a day or so.

"Listen to that," Grandpa would say. "Just listen to the music of that great bird. Close your eyes, lad, and imagine yourself in the heart of the country."

I'd close my eyes, but I could never imagine the countryside. I suppose because I'd never been there.

I painted a picture of Alfred one night. I mixed red with the brown to get the body colour right, then I painted swirls of blue and green running into each other for the tail.

"That's tremendous," said Grandpa. "You've even got the proud tilt of his head. We must hang this up."

"Not on my clean wall, you won't," said Ma, looking up from mending curtains. "Hang it in your room."

On the Saturday before our visitor was due Ma surprised me by giving me money to go to the matinée in the Odeon. I didn't ask why, I just ran to round up some pals before she changed her mind. I had sixpence and, by going to the fourpenny seats, I had enough left over to buy sweets. It was a John Wayne film with plenty of action and only a couple of love bits, during which we flicked sweet papers up into the beam of light from the projectionist's box.

Ma was polishing the brass on the front door when I got home. She was wearing a red scarf tied turban-style around her head.

"Well, Jimmy," she said, pushing my fringe off my forehead with a hand that smelled of Brasso. "Was it a good film?"

"It was great," I enthused. I liked it when she was in a soft mood. I began to tell her about the film but a neighbour stopped to talk.

"Getting ready for the big visit?" she asked Ma.

"I'll tell you about the pictures later, Ma," I said, moving by her to go indoors.

"Jimmy," began Ma as I stepped into the hall. I half turned and saw a sort of helpless look on her face as the neighbour leaned against the wall, settling in for a long conversation. Probably wanted to tell me to wipe my feet. I looked at the soles of my boots, but they were clean. I ran out the back door to the hen run. The four hens were clucking peacefully and scratching through the straw Grandpa had put down. There was no sign of Alfred.

"Here, Alf. Chuck chuck," I called. Lazy beggar was probably asleep in the hut. We'd had to build a bigger hut since the tea-chest had got too small for the five of them. "Come out, you silly creature. I have a bun for you." I climbed over the wire and looked into the hut, but he wasn't there. I glanced anxiously around, trying not to panic. He couldn't have flown over the wire; Grandpa had got advice on the right height to have it before he put it up. Perhaps Grandpa had taken him to show him off somewhere. He was always bragging to his mates about Alfred the Great. He probably had him down at the pub this minute, stuffing him with tit-bits and causing no end of a stir. "Dear Lord, let Grandpa have him," I breathed as I ran up the stairs to make sure. Grandpa was sitting on the chair beside his bed. There was a smell of drink. He looked up, startled, as I burst in the door.

"Grandpa, where's Alfred? I can't find him. I thought you might have him. He must have got out. Come on, we must find him."

Grandpa rose from the chair and reached towards me. He looked old and strange. I backed away, trying to keep my panic at bay.

"She had it done by the time I got back," he said shakily, as though he'd rehearsed the lines. "Told me to go for a pint for myself, that she had a lot to do and that I'd be under her feet."

"Had what done? What are you talking about, Grandpa? Where's Alfred?"

The implications of what he was saying hit me like a blow. I ran down the stairs.

"Wait, Jimmy," Grandpa called, but I ignored him and ran out to the yard. I pulled open the shed door and found Alfred. He was hanging by his feet from a hook on the wall, his eyes closed and blood dripping from his beak on to newspaper which was spread on the floor.

"Oh no! Oh Christ no!" I cried and snatched him from his gallows. His body was still warm and I cradled him in my arms, willing him back to life.

"Leave it, lad." Grandpa touched my shoulder and I jerked away, causing the cock's broken neck to flop across my arm. Alfred was well and truly dead. By now Ma had joined us. Her face registered the horror of what she had done.

7

"Jimmy," she began.

"Why did you do this?" I sobbed, still cradling the lifeless bird. "Why did you have to kill him?" Because I could see that she was sorry I became fearlessly assertive. "You were jealous because I loved him more than I love you. Well, I did and I always will. I hate you," I snarled. "You spoil everything. I really hate you." I buried my face in the cock's plumage and wished that I could die too.

"Easy, lad." Grandpa took the dead bird from me and helped me to my feet. Ma was in tears now. She stretched a hand towards me, but I pushed her away.

"I did it for the best," she said weakly. "I meant well."

"You meant well!" I exploded. "You killed the thing that I loved – that Grandpa and me loved, and you meant well!"

"Take it easy, Jimmy," Grandpa said soothingly, and he put his arm around Ma's shoulder. "It'll be all right," he said to her.

"You're siding with her!" I cried angrily. "She killed our Alfred and you're siding with her. You're as bad as she is."

I wanted to wring both their necks and leave them hanging by their feet, to lock the shed door and go away and never see them again. I ran up to my room and wiped my eyes and nose on the bed-cover. It wasn't really my room. Grandpa and I shared the larger of the two bedrooms, but Ma had made a curtain which effectively divided the room in two. I knelt on my bed and looked out the window at the backyards and labyrinth of lanes which stretched in higgledy-piggledy patterns of grey. Somewhere out there was a world where people didn't have to kill the things they loved. The dreams we had dreamt through Alfred disappeared like spit on candyfloss. I tore down the painting I'd done and crumpled it into a ball.

I pretended not to hear Grandpa's wheezing entry; he always got like that when he moved any faster than his usual shuffle.

"She really did mean well," he said, and I felt the weight

shift as he sat on my bed. "She wants to impress this uncle with a fine meal. She thinks . . . she thinks he'll be able to help you to get on later, when you're older. That he'll be able to take you away from all this and give you a chance to make something of yourself."

I didn't answer. I licked away a tear that had reached the corner of my mouth.

"That's why she wants to give him a day to remember. You can't do that with half a pound of mince or a fatty stew. Try to understand, Jimmy. It's for you she did it." We sat in silence for a few minutes. Then Grandpa sighed and shuffled out, closing the door softly.

It broke my heart to see Alfred stuffed and buttered, ready for the oven.

"I won't eat a scrap of it," I said to Grandpa.

"Me neither," he said, washing the anti-woodwormed cupboard smell off the good china. The kitchen table had been brought into the front room, a neighbour's white table-cloth spread over it. The hope jug had been emptied to buy fiddly little extras. There were paper napkins neatly folded in each set place and a rose in a small vase graced the centre. The room looked foreign and unfamiliar. Grandpa paced uncomfortably in his Sunday suit and white shirt with the stiff collar.

"Why can't I meet him as I normally am?" he pleaded. "I don't want this fellow to think that I go around like this all the time."

"You must look your best," insisted Ma. "First impressions matter. And please," she added, "please keep your teeth in."

Grandpa pursed his lips to accommodate the hated dentures.

Alfred sizzled, the potatoes simmered, the clock ticked and Ma fussed. She had been up since all hours giving the place a final cleaning. "Comb your hair," she said to me.

"I've done it twice already," I protested.

"Well, do it again. He'll be here any moment."

"Here he comes," said Grandpa, standing at the window.

"Come away from the window," whispered Ma. "We don't want him to think that we've been looking out for him."

"And what have we been doing for the past three hours?" Grandpa rolled his eyes heavenward and followed her to the door.

The car which pulled up outside was not the big, pretentious car we'd expected, but a hired Morris Eight. Nevertheless, it was a car and, in the fifties in our street, that was a rarity. Ma glanced proudly along the street where she knew the neighbours would be watching the arrival of our important visitor. The driver's door opened and a small, thin man got out. His pale grey suit was creased. He wore thick, round glasses that made his eyes look owlish. From where we stood at the door, Grandpa and I watched him embrace Ma.

"So, that's the big, important Yank," snorted Grandpa, who'd never met him before, even though he was his brother-in-law. "Did I have to dress up for that little runt?" He gave a suppressed guffaw and nudged me in the back.

Uncle Joe sat in the best armchair, nursing a sherry in a borrowed glass, and gazed at us myopically. Talk was forced and I knew Grandpa was disappointed he hadn't been offered a big cigar, something which we'd associated with rich Americans. This one didn't even smoke a cigarette.

"You'll excuse me now, Uncle Joe," Ma said. "I'll see to dinner."

When we were all seated at the table, she came in bearing the golden brown Alfred on a serving dish. She looked at me as she placed it on the table. A look of apology. Grandpa caught my eye and nodded to reassure me. I won't cry, I thought. I very definitely will not cry.

"Will you carve, Father?" she looked intently at Grandpa. Father! I'd never heard her call him that before. Grandpa hesitantly took the carving knife and gazed for a moment at

Alfred. Then, touched by Ma's sense of ceremony, he turned to our guest.

"Are you a leg or a breast man?" he asked.

Uncle Joe spread a bony hand over his plate and looked up over his glasses at Grandpa.

"Not for me, thank you," he said. "No meat. I'm a vegetarian."

"Huh?" Grandpa's mouth dropped open. He looked at our guest and then looked at Alfred, the carving knife and fork poised. A look of anger crossed his face. "This bird," he began. "If you knew . . . " He stopped, sat down and smiled. "Me too," he said. "I'm a vegetarian too. Me and Jim here." I didn't know what a vegetarian was, but if Grandpa said I was one then it must be OK. "What about yourself?" he asked Ma.

I could see that Ma was perplexed. I wanted to shout at her that she'd killed Alfred for nothing and that I hated her even more. Her face softened as she looked at me again, and I understood. With her shabby green dress which had been ironed so much that it shone, and the borrowed crockery and table-cloth and the impressive meal, this was her practical way of trying to fulfil a different set of dreams for me. She touched my hand and smiled. "I think I'll stick with the vegetables too," she said.

Alfred lay untouched on the table all during the dinner. Like an extra guest.

We saw Uncle Joe off later that evening. Grandpa put his teeth in his pocket as the car disappeared down the street, and looked at the box of chocolates Ma was holding. She'd brought them into the street so that the neighbours would see that our guest had not come empty-handed.

"A miserable box of chocolates," Grandpa grunted.

Ma chuckled. "I wouldn't mind but he ate most of them himself."

Grandpa and I buried Alfred, stuffing and all, in the soft bit of ground beside the ash-pit. Ma gave us a daffodil to plant over him.

SPOTS

Mary Beckett

"Daddy, Mr Jackson says will you water his horrible old loganberries while he's away on holidays?" Angela said.

"What?" her father said because he often didn't listen. Her mother was serving the dinner.

"Angela, wash your hands before you sit down," she said. "And of course we'll water Mr Jackson's garden. But there's no need to be so vociferous."

"I just hate him," Angela said.

"Stop acting like a small child," her mother said. "Why on earth would you hate a harmless old man? You should learn to be more reasonable now you're going to do your 'Junior'."

"He's not a harmless old man," Angela said. "He's horrible – just like his loganberries."

"What is wrong with him, except he's old?" her younger brother asked.

"You can't say people are horrible without putting up some reason," her older brother said.

"What did he do to you?" her mother asked and the table stayed quiet.

"Nothing," Angela answered. "He just asked me to tell Daddy to do the watering."

"There's more to it than that. There must be," her mother said, looking at Angela's face, red with embarrassment.

"Leave me alone," Angela said. She wanted to leave the table and run up to her room, but she knew her mother

12

would make her come back; even at her age her mother had great power.

"What did he say to you?" her mother demanded. "Never mind the watering. What did he say to you that you didn't like? We have to know."

"It doesn't matter," Angela said, shaking her head, wishing her face wasn't burning.

"Listen, Angela," her mother said. "Your dinner is going cold. So is mine. Your father and brothers have, of course, cleared their plates and are waiting for their dessert, so could you please tell me what did Mr Jackson say? We can't just forget your outburst. You know that."

"It's nothing to do with anybody but me," Angela said. "But if you really want to know he peered right into my face and he said "What's wrong with your face? You're all spots.""

And then Angela put her handkerchief up to her eyes and left the kitchen and nobody called her back.

"Goodness, what a fuss," her father said. "I thought it was some of this child abuse."

"She's not a child any longer, Frank, although you might not have noticed. But it was abuse. He had no right," her mother said.

"We'll wreck his loganberries," the older boy said, running his fingers over his own face which, gratefully, was still smooth. "And hack up his grass," his younger brother supported him with enthusiasm.

"You'll do nothing of the sort," their mother said, dividing raspberry shortbread and leaving some aside for Angela.

"Frank will water Mr Jackson's garden and none of you will go near it. I mean that now – both of you."

"What can we do to him?" asked the younger boy.

"You can be polite and pleasant to him and realise that sometimes old people forget that young people have feelings," their mother said and then added, "You will also remember to be considerate with Angela. Even if you are fighting with her you are *never* to mention her skin."

The two boys escaped out to play with their friends, leaving the kitchen door open. Angela, in her own room, was examining with distaste her face in the mirror. Her fingers travelled up and down her cheeks, and then to her chin where they pounced viciously to squeeze and pick at a slight rise under her skin until it turned fiery red. Both hands then attacked her forehead till a trickle of blood ran down the outside of her eyebrow. She paused to listen to her parents downstairs.

"I don't know where those spots of Angela's come from. Do you, Valerie?" her father said.

"It's ordinary enough for teenagers. I'll see about it now I see she's so upset. It's not really bad – I thought it best to take no notice. But I was wrong," her mother said.

"There never were any spots in our family," her father said and her mother answered "Oh, we know all that. There never was anything short of perfection in your family. I don't know how your children will live up to that. Your family were thorough-bred Glenmoy raspberries – each one glossy, perfumed, immaculate. My family were just ordinary old wild blackberries. We were never worthy of you. You have to be satisfied with blackberries as offspring."

Her father laughed. He didn't mind her mother saying things like that. He even seemed to enjoy it. Maybe, Angela thought, he believed she meant it.

She returned to punishing her face and was so intent on it that she jumped when her mother appeared beside her.

"Angela," she said. "I'll bring you to the doctor's, I'll buy you good cosmetics, but what can I do if you insist on ruining yourself?"

"Me! What am I doing?" Angela said, turning her face

down towards an open drawer and pretending to hunt for something.

"I'll tell you something," her mother said. "Your skin looks a lot worse now than when Mr Jackson insulted you. You'd frighten the poor man now with the blood running down your forehead."

Angela found a tissue and scrubbed indiscriminately at her face. Then she turned to her mother with her chin in the air.

"Don't you realise it's a compulsion? I can't stop."

"I don't care if it's an addiction, Angela; you can stop if you have any self-respect. Your father used to smoke forty cigarettes a day and he stopped before you were born and never smoked again so that he could do well for his children."

All the family had been told that story, time and time again, by their mother. Their father never mentioned smoking.

"All right, now," her mother went on. "You'll cut your nails as short as possible."

"Maybe I should *bite* my nails like Emma Louise," Angela said, in order to be cheeky. She wanted her mother to go away and leave her alone.

"Let's hope the stress of choosing between wrecked nails and wrecked skin doesn't damage you," her mother said. She never reacted properly to her children's impertinence, Angela thought. She had heard of other girls' mothers who had refused to speak to them for days because of a disagreement.

Angela understood that she only had her friends' account, that she didn't have their mothers' versions. The stories were told with such gusto Angela doubted them. She thought it would be satisfactory if some of her barbed remarks would obviously hurt her mother, but it would be awkward if they were enemies. Angela didn't know if perhaps she was not yet grown-up enough to find a sensitive spot. Or was her mother immune? And how did one become immune?

"Your nail scissors?" Her mother was looking at the clutter on her dressing-table. "No time like the present. And then an emery board to smooth away anything that can do damage. Of course I would suggest finding a use for your hands – like embroidery or sewing or making a rug – but I know what you'd say."

"I'd like tatting," Angela said, deciding that it was wise to go along with her mother's determination.

"When I was young," her mother said "some girls smoked so as to have something to do with their hands. Thank goodness your friends are more self-assured. It was a bit pathetic, don't you think?"

Angela said nothing. She had never smoked, never would. But some of her friends did and she wasn't going to talk about them. She began to trim her nails.

"Tomorrow," her mother said, "I'll give you the money to get some of that cream from the chemist that's supposed to cure and cover."

"Couldn't you get it for me?" Angela said. "I hate people looking at my face."

"I will if you want me to," her mother said, "but if people are really looking at you they are saying to themselves, 'Hasn't that girl got a pretty face, if she'd only brush her hair away from it.' Normally people don't look much. Their eyes glance over."

"Oh, you have no idea what it feels like," Angela said. "If I'm in a restaurant and I see somebody across the room looking at me, I feel like hiding down under the table."

Her mother looked at her steadily so that she could feel the blush rising again. "I think, Angela, you are exaggerating. I don't know that you frequent restaurants greatly. But you are a teenager with troubled skin. You are lucky that you are straight and slim. Some of your classmates are overweight, which is much more obvious. However, next week I'll make an appointment with an Elizabeth Arden counter in town and you will present yourself – if you can summon your courage. You can be shown how to do the best possible camouflage and we'll buy whatever I agree is sensible even though it will be expensive. Then you'll use it until it's finished – no chopping and changing with cheap stuff hidden away in drawers."

"Mammy, I don't," Angela protested automatically.

"And when all that is accomplished we can, if you like, go to the doctor and see what tablets he'd give you. But I think that would be a last resort. Now do you feel better about it?" her mother asked.

"Oh, yes," Angela said.

"So wash your face and come downstairs for your dessert. And for goodness sake *do* keep your fingers away from your skin." She tapped Angela lightly on the shoulder.

The dinner dishes were waiting to be washed so Valerie ran the hot water and Frank lifted the tea-towel automatically.

"You could have washed these while I was up dealing with Angela," Valerie said.

"Indeed I could. I'm sorry. I never thought," Frank said.

Angela had said that he should have "I never thought" engraved on his tombstone but he only said he was going to be cremated.

The younger boy said goodbye to his friends on the doorstep, looked into the kitchen to say "I'm in, Mammy" and turned on the television in the sitting-room. Angela came downstairs and carried her dessert in to join him. She was back in the kitchen, adding her empty dish to her parents' work and mooching about, aware she was still hungry, when the other brother came in and said,

"Do you know what I heard about Mr Jackson?"

His mother turned round to face him.

17

"Surely, Eamonn, you did not go out there talking about Mr Jackson! How many times have we told you not to repeat outside what you hear in the house!"

"No, no, I didn't," Eamonn said. "I didn't say a word. I just *heard* something."

"Well, go on," his mother said dubiously.

"We were sitting on the wall down at the corner," he began.

"Who were?" Angela asked.

"Me and Damien and Dominic," he answered "but that doesn't matter. We were just sitting there. I know some women think we're going to jump on them and steal their handbags but we're not. Two women from the avenue were standing talking to Mrs Keegan and one of them mentioned Mr Jackson so I listened."

"Well?" said his mother.

"Well, they said that Mr Jackson had just had a laser operation on his eye. That he'd been half-blind for a long time until he got this done. So I thought that's why he peered into Angela's face. He didn't mean to be rude." He grew less sure of himself with every word. "That's all anyway."

"And what does he see but spots before his eyes?" their father said and their mother groaned "Oh, Frank" in despair.

Angela stood still. Her father turned towards her and winked confidentially. She began to laugh and went on laughing and Eamonn laughed with her in relief. Her mother put her arm round her shoulders and hugged her.

"Angela, you are a great girl. Never think anything else. You'll cope with anything big or small. And you'll have years of pink and white winters and golden summers before the wrinkles come. You'll be a lovely laughing girl. You'll forget you ever met old Mr Jackson."

But she wouldn't.

UNEVEN GROUND

Michael Carroll

When I was in first year there was a kid in most of my classes called Derek Murphy. He was my age – thirteen – and a bit shorter than me, though that doesn't mean anything because at that time everyone in the class was growing like crazy. One week someone would be the tallest, the next week it would be someone else.

He was only with us for first year, and I never got to know him well, but the thing I remember most about Derek was that he was probably the fastest runner in the history of the school. He didn't care for most sports, but running was something he loved. On the days when the PE teacher didn't feel up to supervising a mad group of future Liverpool players attempting to play offside for an entire match, she used to just make us run around the pitch, and Derek said he loved that more than anything.

I wasn't much of a runner myself, so I was usually last, especially if we had to do more than five laps. Derek was always – and I mean *always* – first. By the time I was panting and gasping near the end of the first lap, Derek was usually more than half-way into the second. A lap later, and he'd passed me.

He wasn't much good at anything else, though. Derek's attendance was terrible – that's one of the reasons I can't remember too much about him – and for such a fast runner he was usually late for PE. That's probably because our PE class was held the first thing every Tuesday morning. None of us were very enthusiastic about it. We'd all be standing there in a line on the playing field, either freezing our backsides off or getting sunstroke, while the teacher droned on about aerobic exercise or something, when Derek would come charging over from the gym, skid to a stop at the end of the line, and not even be out of breath.

On the first day back after Christmas, Derek was late again. The teacher, Mrs Henry, looked at her watch. "Right," she said, slapping her hands together. "It's a cold day out, but at least it's dry. You'll warm up when you run around a bit."

We all groaned. The kid in line next to me muttered that he'd asked Santa for a fur-lined tracksuit, but instead all he got was a couple of records. I laughed at this, and next thing I knew Mrs Henry was roaring at me:

"*Mis*ter Carroll! Since you're in such a good mood, you can lead the way!" She pointed towards the gym door.

I slouched over to the door. It was one of those fire escape doors, with a long locking bar instead of a handle. I knew from past experience that the bar would be freezing. I gripped the bar, pulled it down, and pushed open the door. An icy gale tore into the gym, and everyone – except the teacher, who wasn't actually human – shivered.

It took some effort to pull my hands free of the bar: I'd already had them half-frozen on the way to school because the shoulder straps on my bag had broken before Christmas, and I'd had to carry the bag by the handle. I did have gloves, of course, but they'd been in the schoolbag and my hands had been too cold to open the clasp. So everyone trundled out past me. Since I was the Duly Appointed Official Door Opener, I had to wait until they were all out before I closed the door behind me. As Mrs Henry herded the rest of the boys up to the field, I started wondering how two entire weeks off could have gone by so fast, and what I had done in my past life to warrant such torture.

Derek arrived at the gym's school door as I was about to close up the outer door. "Hey! Derek!" I called.

He looked over to me, and gave me one of those sad smiles. "Aw no! Not outside *again*!"

"Yeah," I said. "Eight hundred laps around the field. You'd better hurry."

I closed the door behind me and half-ran to catch up with the others. There hadn't really been any need to tell Derek to hurry, because none of the teachers ever gave out to him for being late. I knew that they thought he was such a brilliant runner that he'd eventually win lots of medals for the school.

Of course, we didn't know then that he wasn't going to come back at the end of first year, and we certainly didn't know that he was going to win two gold medals and a bronze eight years later in the European Championships. And I keep telling myself that there was no way we could have known what was going on in Derek's mind all the time he was with us.

But then, he was never really *with* us: he was there, occasionally, but he was always outside the group. At lunch and recess we'd often be sitting around in the lobby, telling jokes and wild, untrue stories. Derek would just sit and listen; laughing with the rest of us, but never contributing.

Apart from his running, Derek never took part in things. A few weeks after we'd started in the school, when we were still only finding our way around and still sorting out friendships, I tried to talk to him. Like me, all of his friends from primary school had gone to other places, so he knew no one. I sat next to him in the library, and tried to talk about something that had been on TV the previous night.

But he wasn't interested. "We don't have a telly at home," Derek said. "My mother's got a nervous condition, and television just makes things worse."

"So what do you do?"

He shrugged. "We read, mostly. We're a fairly quiet family, most of the time."

I'd guessed that much. I was about to ask him what sort of books he read, when he pointed to my bare arm.

"Where'd you get the bruises?"

I glanced down at my arm, and laughed. "Watch!" I licked my finger, then rubbed at the bruise. It began to spread. "It's just blue biro. You draw a little dot, lick your finger and rub it around. If you do it right, it looks like a bruise and you can get out of PE. It works best if you do it on a bump that's already there."

Derek laughed. "Well, PE's my favourite class, so I wouldn't want to do that."

That was when he told me about his running. His parents had owned a farm, but times were tough and they'd been forced to sell and move to the suburbs. Derek said he learned to run while on the farm.

"I can run faster than a tractor," he said with a smile. "That's why I'm much faster running over uneven ground than I am on tarmac or concrete." He paused, then added, "But if I'm ever going to be a professional athlete, I suppose I'll have to learn to run on a track."

I'd already seen Derek run, so I knew how good he was. But at the age of thirteen, I was still under the impression that we could all become famous for something. A couple of years later I was destined to be a legendary rock guitarist, and after that an action movie star, then a karate champion. So to me it seemed the most natural thing in the world that Derek would become a star on the track. And, of course, he did.

As far as I know, he's the only student ever to come out of the school who went on to become a household name.

But that day, the first day back after the Christmas break, Derek was longer than usual appearing on the field. Mrs Henry had half of us doing press-ups on the frozen ground, while the other half were running on the spot.

When Derek arrived, it wasn't at his usual pace. Instead, he was walking rather stiffly. Mrs Henry gave him another one of those looks but she didn't say anything. Had we been older, I suppose it might have occurred to us that they were having an affair or something. She never gave him any hassle: Derek was quiet enough as it was, there was no need to make their future star athlete any more self-conscious.

As it happened, Derek ended up next to me in line when it was our turn to run on the spot. He was still moving stiffly, so for a change I was just about able to keep up with him.

When Mrs Henry moved to inspect the other end of the line, I asked him what was up.

He stopped, and stared at me, as though I'd stumbled onto his darkest secret. "What do you mean?"

"Well, you're not your usual self. You know, you're all stiff and awkward."

For a second, I thought he was going to cry. "I fell off my bike a few days before Christmas. Hurt my back really bad." He hesitated, then said, "I don't know if I'll ever be able to run properly again."

"Jesus! Did you break anything?"

Derek looked at me as though I was being stupid, which I suppose I was. "If I'd broken something, I don't think I'd be here now."

I laughed. "Oh, right. Didn't think of that."

Then the teacher decided that we'd warmed up enough, and we should have enough time for a couple of slow laps around the field. She turned to Derek, and said, "And this isn't a race, Mr Murphy. Don't go charging off in front like you usually do."

As we ran, I kept up with Derek. "Didn't you tell her that you'd hurt your back?"

"No. It doesn't matter, anyway. I'll probably be fine in a couple of weeks."

He did seem to be moving with a bit more ease now, so I let the matter drop.

After the couple of laps – which as usual meant about six – we headed back to the gym to shower and change. In the shower, I noticed the mass of scars and bruises on Derek's back. Derek said that he'd crashed the bike pretty bad: he'd hit a pothole, the front wheel had buckled and he'd been thrown over the handlebars, landing hard on his back.

He was sort of laughing about it as he told me, though. "I suppose it might have been better if I'd gone under a bus," he said. But then he was suddenly serious. "At least then it wouldn't hurt any more."

That wasn't the first time I'd heard anyone suggest that death might be a good alternative, but it was the first time that I'd ever heard anyone sound as if they meant it. A few days later, I thought about what he'd said and it hit me hard, a lot harder than I realised at first.

It was Friday night, and as usual our parents had gone out, and we were allowed to stay up late. My brother and sister were downstairs, fighting over the television and using the old "I was sitting there" argument, when out of the blue it occurred to me that Derek and his family must never have that sort of argument.

And that made me wonder what his family life was like. Over the few months I'd known him, I'd built up the impression that they were as obsessed with running as he was, but now it occurred to me that maybe it wasn't like that at all. Maybe Derek's parents pushed him into doing it, maybe they hoped that he'd make it as a professional and be able to support them – Derek had mentioned that his father still hadn't found a job.

The more I thought about it, the more I realised that his home life must be a nightmare. I knew that he went running every night for at least an hour, regardless of the weather, and that he ran with a club every Saturday and Sunday morning.

When I remembered what he'd said about how it might have been better if he had died, I knew that he hated running. He wanted it to end. He was his family's only hope and the pressure was getting too much for him.

I spent the rest of the year not knowing what to do or say to him. After a few weeks, his injuries healed and soon he was able to run at least as well as before. We even had a relay race in school, and Derek wasn't partnered: he ran the whole race on his own, and won.

Of course, as it turned out, I was wrong about Derek's hatred for running.

It wasn't until I was eighteen, with school long behind me, that I learned the true story.

That was when Derek became famous for the first time. His European Championship medals were still in the future. He'd won a couple of minor races, but he didn't take part in many competitions.

I hadn't seen him since the end of first year, and it never occurred to me to get in touch. Even if I had known how to, I don't think I would have bothered. I had my own life to live and I rarely thought about him.

On his eighteenth birthday, Derek became famous when he came close to beating his father to death. Derek's solicitor pleaded mitigating circumstances, and the rest of Derek's family supported him. The papers told of how Mr Murphy had been beating his wife and children for years. Derek's father was a chronic alcoholic. He'd been forced to sell the farm, he'd been unable to keep a job, and he took out his frustrations on his family.

When I read the story, I remembered the scars and bruises on Derek's back, where they didn't show. I remembered how none of the teachers ever gave him any trouble for being late. And I remembered how he said he'd learned to run on the farm.

Now, whenever I remember him, I don't see him as the thirteen-year-old who could beat an entire relay team. I don't see him as the kid who always arrived late, skidding to a stop when he reached the rest of us. All I can see is a terrified young boy, running for his life across an open field, with tears streaming down his face and the deafening roar of a tractor close behind.

THE OLD DOG

Marita Conlon-Mckenna

Whisky was my father's dog. That was plain for all to see, as the brindled coloured mongrel's eyes would follow his every move. She was constantly trying to side-step his heavy, polished, black leather shoes and keep out of his way. Yet, when he called or whistled for her, she would rise from her haunches and, shaking her long shaggy coat, come to the back door and follow him down the pathway, throwing us a wild-eyed look which was a mixture of self-loathing and pride, as she accompanied him on his journey, up the town, across the fields or down by the river, leaving us behind.

My father was a big man, twice the man that any of his sons would ever be. He cut a handsome figure, attired in his heavy brown tweed or his grey flannel, for summer and winter he always chose to wear a suit. He was well respected and liked by the neighbours and the town, for he had a way with figures, and his knowledge of business matters and insurance was much sought after. He understood the vagaries of farm life and the tide of money, in and out, which affected the whole locality. He alone seemed to know when a man could afford to pay an insurance premium or not.

Whisky had been acquired by him during a visit to Tom Taafe's farm, more than twelve years ago. Tom had told him that his beloved Netty, a collie bitch, had given birth to five mixed-blood, useless pups, a few nights before. Tom, wanting rid of them, had tied them up in a sack. Four had drowned and, much to his disbelief, the runt of the litter had managed to survive and had emerged on the river-bank sodden and miserable, as her brothers and sisters were swept downstream to their fate.

So my father had taken the unwanted pup, and on arrival home ordered my mother to keep it warm and feed it. All night my mother sat, coaxing the pup to drink a mixture of warmed milk and my father's golden liquid. He raged and threatened about the waste of his precious alcohol, but grudgingly had to admit that the whisky had probably saved the young dog's life. My brothers and I loved the pup and longed to play with Whisky, as she had been christened, but our father made it quite clear to us that the pup was not to be mollycoddled, and was not to be considered a house dog. Whisky was his dog.

He trained the pup, using a willow switch to admonish her. The dog cowered and hid at the sound of his voice, and gobbled and gulped at the few scraps of food he would use to reward her. My mother would secretly feed her with bits of leftovers and the old sweet biscuit, talking to her gently at the back door, while we kept an eye out for my father.

She slept on an old blanket in the corner of the woodhouse. We would cry and beg my father to let her in when winter gales blew around the house and hailstones battered against the window panes, but he just ignored our pleas and told us gruffly to get on with our homework!

Inside our home my father rarely spoke, except to tell us our faults and urge us to study or work harder. He didn't like disturbance when he tried to concentrate and read the daily paper, or settle down to his correspondence. My mother had her hands full trying to deal with a houseful of growing boys who never wanted to be quiet or good. We could see the frown of worry and the line of tension around her mouth which disappeared when he left the house and set off for work doing his insurance rounds or across the fields with his shooting gun strapped to his shoulder and the dog at his heels.

As we got older, however, my father's insurance rounds seemed to get smaller and smaller, as neighbours began to post cheques and to deal with corporate stangers. He became more taciturn, ignoring my mother's remarks that the housekeeping money wouldn't stretch to cover the cost of jackets and shoes and trousers, which we were constantly growing out of or wearing out. For once she thanked heaven that she had no daughter. How could she have denied pretty dresses and patent shoes and fancy dolls and the like to a little girl? My father cursed her constant whining and trying to get money from him.

My eldest brother, Jim, left home at sixteen, taking the boat to England. My father was deeply disappointed that a son of his would work as a common labourer on an English building site, but I knew well that Jim had had enough of the "old man" and wanted to get away. He'd hugged my mother, ignoring her tears, shaking my hand and patting Whisky on the head as he said his goodbyes. My brother Donal followed him across the Irish Sea two years later. The "old man" would barely mention their names, though I noticed him watching for the daily post, and he read and re-read their letters to our mother over and over again.

I was now the eldest at home. My father urged me to study and attended every football match that I played for the school. He made it clear that he would not countenance my following the brothers. All he could talk of was my exams. He was filled with expectations for my future.

My father had become an old man, even shrinking in size, so it seemed to me, for I could now look him square in the eye, though he could still tower over my mother and my younger brothers. He rarely spoke to my mother, expect to question her over housekeeping money or to determine the whereabouts of some item of clothing. My mother bore it all, trying to maintain her good humour and taking joy in us, her sons. She rarely argued with him.

The old dog was also showing signs of her long canine years, and my mother had insisted that Whisky finally be taken from the dark, cold, damp woodshed and be let have a bed near the range, where her old arthritic bones could enjoy some bit of heat. My father's attempts to object were overruled and he grudgingly gave in to the dog sitting in the kitchen with us.

Whisky no longer barked when a stranger approached our home, and my mother pitied the dog's obvious loss of hearing. Sitting at the table with us all, my father would at times pass a stringy piece of bacon fat or a bit of gristly beef down to the waiting dog. He would even give her the odd pat as he sipped his mug of tea. We brothers wondered if, perhaps, at last the old man was softening. How and ever, despite the warmth of the kitchen and the extra attention, it was clear that the dog was sick. Every so often a shudder seemed to run through her, and Whisky would almost topple over. Even in her sleep, shudders involuntarily rippled down her spine and through the golden coat.

"The dog needs to go to the vet," suggested my mother, but my father would have none of it. He had fallen out with Bill McGrath, the local vet, a few years back over his failure to renew a substantial policy and had sworn never to do business with him again. So we boys were left watching my mother's attempts to relieve the dog's suffering.

I had had enough of it and one sunny October day I called Whisky to come for a walk with me. The dog ambled slowly behind as we walked through the fallen leaves, stopping to sniff at musky autumnal smells and every now and then taking the chance to rest herself. It grieved me to see her so . . . once she had raced and jumped along this familar route, joyous with the sounds and smells of the open air.

We stopped by the river-bank. The river was swollen after the week's rain, the rushy edges slippy and damp. Whisky stood beside me. I sensed her fear as the waters raged by us. I walked on. After a while I realised that she had quit follwing me. I doubled back to find her lying in a curve of bracken, panting, tongue lolling out, as those wretched shudders wracked her body. Her paws stretched stiffly towards me. She whimpered as I tried to stroke her. "'Tis all right girl!" I tried to reassure her, unable to take the look in her eyes. I turned my back to her and, unstrapping the gun, loaded it. I raised my father's hunting gun, lodging it against my shoulder, the way I'd seen him do it; then stepping back a few paces from her, I took slow and careful aim. I prayed she would not rise up and come towards me. Whisky was no longer interested in the hunt. My finger caught the heavy trigger, pulling it, the force almost punching my shoulder. I lowered the gun . . . For an instant she had seemed bewildered, betrayed, but now she lay totally still, her head resting against her shabby coat. I felt only relief that she was out of this life that had treated her so cruelly, ever since she was a young pup. Patting her soft fur for the last time, I left her lying there, amidst the fronds of bracken and the blood-stained ground, and, unloading the gun, turned for home. I felt old and very weary.

My mother was waiting at the back door. They had heard the shot. My little brother Mickey was crying, and my brother Patrick greeted me with a mighty kick.

"You're a murderer!" he screamed, ignoring my mother's pleas to leave me alone. Then we all sat waiting . . .

My father arrived home at his regular time, and sat down at the table with us for his tea. My mother had made a beef stew, one of his favourite dishes. He ate slowly, relishing it. Mickey left a piece of his meat on the plate.

"Give it to the dog," suggested my father.

Mickey looked startled, ready to cry. The old man's glance flew around the kitchen, under the table, to her spot near the range. He knew at once that we were all hiding something from him. His gaze rested on my mother.

"The dog's dead, Frank," she said softly.

"I killed her!" The words shot out of me. "She was in pain! I couldn't stick it any longer so I took her down by the river and shot her. I put her out of her misery."

He did not answer, but got up from the table and went out to the hall press to inspect his gun. "You young pup! You are not let touch that gun!" he roared angrily at me, "I've told you often enough not to go near my things. How dare you take my gun!"

He made to shake me but my mother came between us.

"Frank, he was only thinking of the poor dog. He's a kind boy."

My father returned to his meal, adding another floury potato to his dinner plate. We all sat silent.

"Did you bury the dog?" he asked after a long time.

I shook my head.

"Then you'd better finish the job you started," he added sarcastically. "Bury her."

I nodded, watching him mash his gravy and potato together.

"Else the rats will get her."

I'd fetch the shovel and her old blanket when we'd finished our meal.

He ate slowly, knowing that my mother was waiting to serve the rice pudding.

"Johnny Quinlan's dog had pups about a month ago," he said aloud. "I've a mind to go down and take a look at them tomorrow."

Young Mickey's eyes lit up at the thought of a new pup. I thought of the bloody bundle of fur that I would bury later.

As I dug deep into that damp river-strained earth, I thought of my brothers, Jim and Donal, forgotten too. They had urged me to join them in London where they were building a business for themselves.

My mother would cry. But now I was too old to stay.

31

THE VISIT

June Considine

It began to rain as the train pulled out of Heuston Station. A dull drizzle that slicked the railway tracks and filled the carriage with the wet-wool smell of overcoats. The train window steamed but Keith didn't bother wiping it. The country was a bore. A hole in the earth where nothing happened. How could his father have settled in such a dead, silent place where even the cows were too lazy to lift their heads as the train sped past?

"Selfishness." He imagined his mother's reply. "Don't try and look for a deeper motive."

Keith wanted to stay out of her anger. It filled him with guilt and a sense of helplessness, the feeling that, somehow, he should have been able to prevent what happened. At night, when he could not sleep, the events that led to his father's departure played over and over in his mind. Like a completed jig-saw puzzle, slotting neatly into place, taunting him . . . if only . . . if only . . .

If only he had not asked Conor Lorcan for a loan of his do-it-yourself book on how to build an aquarium. If only he had not gone to Conor's house to see his collection of exotic fish. If only his father had said straight out, no aquarium, they're too much trouble and you'll forget to clean it out and to feed the fish and they'll die from neglect, bellies up and floating. Keith's father could lay on a lecture with a trowel but on this occasion he decided it was an excellent idea and when he called to collect him from Conor's house he too came in to inspect the aquarium.

It spanned the arch between the two downstairs rooms. A glass partition where fish with spiky heads and tails like feathers flashed between fronds of seaweed and miniature beds of coral. Looking after the aquarium kept her son out of mischief, said Conor's mother. Whenever Keith tried to picture her that night he could only remember her sleek red hair and the way she laughed when his father said it was important for teenagers to have another interest in life besides listening to music that sounded like trains being hammered into scrap metal.

Keith wondered who made the first phone call. Who suggested the first meeting? Was it accidental or planned? Deliberate intent? A whim of fate? These things were important to know but who could he ask?

"We didn't expect it to happen." When the lies were finally uncovered and decisions made his father tried to explain the impossible. "Neither of us wanted to be the cause of so much unhappiness. But love is a strange emotion, Keith. It eats into your heart. It takes you over and nothing makes sense unless you are together. Some day, when you're older, you'll understand."

"I'll never understand," Keith shouted. "If I live to be a million years old I'll never understand how you could do this to us."

His father's hangdog expression and abject explanations could not hide his anticipation. He was beginning a new life. sloughing off the old one as if it counted for nothing. As if love was some sort of crazy madness, stronger even than the fourteen years he had shared with his son.

Keith hated him so much that shivers ran under his skin whenever letters arrived with a Kerry postmark. They were torn into pieces without being opened. The phone calls were also ignored and when Keith hung up without speaking he felt a vicious sense of satisfaction because this was something he could control.

The first visit had been arranged for his October mid-term break. His mother was going to Greece for a week with a man called Barry who wore leather trousers and was, she said, helping to put her life back together again. Keith did not want to visit his father. But in the end he allowed himself to be persuaded. He did not know if he was ready to forgive. Or if he was just tired feeling guilty.

His father's appearance had changed dramatically in the ten months since they had seen each other. A silver-looped earring hung from one ear and his hair was long enough to be tied in a ponytail. Jeans, a crumpled wax jacket and muddy wellingtons replaced the once-familiar grey suit, the black leather shoes. A beard hid the soft outline of a double chin. It gave his face a rough, craggy look, reminding Keith of hermits and men who drank wine in doorways.

"Hey, what's with the fuzz?" he asked, pulling his fingers in a downward stroke over his chin.

"No time for shaving down here," said his father. "Easier to let it grow. That's the best thing about being your own boss. No one tells you what to do."

Keith flung his backpack into the boot of the car where strips of bark and moss and splintered tree trunks were piled to one side. "Still whittling wood?" he asked, climbing into the passenger seat.

"Don't speak to me in your mother's voice, Keith." His father frowned and touched his earring as if suddenly conscious of its presence. "I know these past months haven't been easy for you . . . for any of us. That's why this week is so important. We'll have time to talk, get everything out in the open. Gloves off." His car was an arrow on the bends, not slowing, skidding once on the wet surface. They came to a harbour, just a pier and some old rusting trawlers. His father stopped the car and blasted the horn three times. "Where is he? He's supposed to be here to meet you."

"Who?"

"Conor, of course. He's forever hanging around this dump." He nodded towards the trawlers and began to tap the steering wheel, his nails beating a hard, rapid tempo that gave way to another blast of the horn, when he noticed an old man climbing the steps of the pier. "Hey, Barney! Have you seen Conor?" he shouted.

"He's out with Jimmy," the old man paused, peering curiously in through the window at Keith. "It'll be late enough when they get back."

"Typical . . . just typical!" The ignition was turned on and they were on the move again. On either side of the road hedgerows knuckled down for the winter. Trees stripped of leaves, others holding a last blaze of colour, stood still and stark against the grey skyline. A tractor blocked their progress and was passed so sharply that Keith gripped the dashboard, closing his eyes against the sudden rush of speed.

"I suppose you're going to adopt him?" he said. "Him and his aquarium."

"Don't be like that, now," his father replied. "You know that Conor will never be a substitute for you. But what could I do? He's Marianne's son. We had to bring him with us."

"What about his own father? Where does *he* figure in all of this?"

"Nowhere. He doesn't want to be saddled with any responsibility. He's in London now . . . having a high old time from what Marianne tells me." His father made no attempt to hide his irritation and it silenced them both until they came to a cottage set in the shadow of a mountain. It was a sturdy, whitewashed building with black wooden beams arching across the living-room ceiling.

"Welcome . . . welcome . . . welcome!" Marianne held him at arm's length, tilting her head to one side. Her teeth were long and white, protruding slightly when she smiled. "Good gracious me, how you've grown. And good-looking

35

too. Just like your father." She waved her hand around the room which had a *Welcome Home, Keith* poster pinned to the wall. "It's good to have you with us at last. Conor's been counting the days."

"I guess he forgot to count this one," snapped Keith's father. "He wasn't at the harbour. God knows when he'll get back tonight. He's doing it deliberately to annoy you."

"He probably forgot," said Marianne, smiling her wide white smile as she led Keith towards his bedroom. "Don't let him upset you so much."

Two single beds in the one room meant that he had to share with Conor. Grimly, he began to unpack, unable to get rid of the feeling that he was trespassing on someone else's space. Yet there was little evidence of Conor's presence. No wall posters or books or CDs. No clutter of clothes on the floor. No aquarium, nor even a small square tank or a goldfish bowl.

They had almost finished their evening meal when Conor returned home.

"What kept you?" his mother demanded. "Keith's been looking forward all evening to seeing you again."

The two boys gazed blankly at each other.

"How's it going?" asked Conor.

"Oh, you know . . . " Keith shrugged and tried to think of something to say. Nothing came to mind. But then they never had talked about much except aquariums and the life cycle of exotic fish.

"Cat got your tongue, Keith?" asked his father.

He stared at his plate and muttered. "Leave it out, will you?"

Conor refused to eat and went straight to his room.

"Boys!" Marianne sighed. "Wouldn't they just break your heart?"

"Keith! Why don't you go up to him?" suggested his father. "Make some effort."

A bottle of red wine glowed warmly on the hearth. Music played on the stereo, high plaintive violins that made Keith's head ache. "Because I want to watch television, that's why," he replied.

He stared fixedly at the screen, ignoring their impatience, their desire to be alone. It was midnight when he went to bed. He undressed in darkness, sliding between the cold sheets. A bed creaked on the other side of the wall. He pulled a pillow over his ears but still he could hear them. Sighing, hushed cries that made his heart race with shock and embarrassment and something else that set his blood on fire because he could imagine them, in there, together, with no clothes on, kissing and whispering secret words to each other and then . . . and then . . .

Before his mind could form any more pictures he jumped from bed and pulled on his clothes. The rain had stopped. A full moon, plump as a melon, hung low in the sky. He remembered the breaking sound of his parents' marriage. The crash of a crystal clock against the mantelpiece. His mother throwing it with such fury that he woke up and ran downstairs. He had watched his father pick up a fragment of glass. A relieved expression on his face. As if the broken shards had released some great and burdensome secret.

"Aren't you able to sleep?" asked Conor.

"I didn't mean to wake you," said Keith, startled at his sudden appearance.

"You didn't." Sparks glowed as Conor flicked cigarette ash into the wind.

"What's it like . . . living with them?"

"It's cool. They let me do my own thing."

"It'd make me sick."

"They don't bother me. I'm out of here as soon as my father gets his own place."

"What's keeping him?"

"He's in London. It's not that easy setting things up."

"It didn't take *them* long."

"So, what are you saying? He doesn't want me?" Conor's voice was a flat monotone. "Just because your old man bunks off without looking backwards doesn't mean mine will do the same."

It didn't hurt. Nothing Conor said could hurt because the enormity of what had happened to them both left no space between them for anything but anger. Above them the mountain blurred into the night and invisible streams surged from sharp granite clefts to begin their twisting journey to the sea. Relics of an ice age. History always left something behind.

In the morning Conor was gone before anyone else was awake. His absence didn't bother Keith, who spent the day watching videos.

"You didn't come all the way to Kerry to sprawl on a sofa," said his father. "Where the hell is Conor? The least he could do is show you around the place."

"And I didn't come all the way to Kerry to be with him, so stop trying to shove us together. When are we going to talk?"

"We will . . . we will. But not today. I'm up to my eyes with work."

In a studio at the side of the cottage Keith's father made montages from wood and dried moss which he sold to tourists, who were fascinated by the strange, stark images of animals and birds. When Keith examined them he was ordered to stop mooching. He was disturbing his father's concentration.

Conor still hadn't returned when Marianne began to prepare their evening meal. The light cast a glow over the polished table and on the pans hanging from the walls. On the window ledge herbs grew from earthenware containers. Tomatoes and peppers were arranged in hand-painted porcelain bowls. The room reminded Keith of a painting,

38

each detail painted with exquisite perfection. Marianne hummed as she worked, making no effort to engage him in conversation. Once she rested her hands almost absent-mindedly on her stomach and when she smiled at Keith he felt as if she was looking at him from a long way off. Rain swept down from the mountain. It blew against the window, creating an intimacy he did not want or feel. He was relieved when the back door opened and Conor entered. His oilskin jacket gleamed with rain and dripped water when he shook it over the floor.

"I was helping the lads bring the catch ashore." He held up a plastic bag filled with mackerel and waggled it in front of his mother's face. "Payment."

She wrinkled her nose and pushed him aside. "You smell like the inside of a trawler. I told you to stop bringing fish into the house."

"It's perfectly good fish," he replied, opening the bag and lifting out a mackerel by its tail. He took a knife and placed the fish on the chopping board. His hands looked raw, as if they had been dipped too long in cold water. "I'll fillet them and put them into the freezer,"

"Get them out of here, Conor. This instant!"

"It'll only take a minute." The belly of the mackerel was slit in a deft sideways stroke. Entrails slid out, a greasy pool of dark blood staining the chopping board and oozing over the table.

"Why must you always spoil everything?" Marianne cried.

Conor ignored her. Keith knew he was spoiling for a fight. He tensed, waiting for it to happen. Blood on the walls. Gloves off, as his father would say. But she turned her back on her son and stirred a saucepan where the careful blending of herbs and spices and simmering chicken was soon swamped under the cloying, oily smell pervading the kitchen.

39

"Satisfied now?" she asked when he had finished stacking the fish into a chest freezer. "Or have you planned anything else to ruin my night?"

"What's the big deal?" said Conor, briskly clearing away the entrails and swabbing the chopping board. "All I did was bring you home some fish and you can't even say 'thank you'."

The weather changed, became mild again, and Keith explored the rocky caves along the shore. His father was busy. He looked harried every time Keith entered the studio. He talked about change. A painful and difficult process. But it was also a challenge. How it was handled was what really mattered. He sounded hearty. The sales pitch he had once used to sell computers. He glanced meaningfully at Keith, who wondered if his father's conversations had always been loaded with such clichés. This man was a stranger. Not because he had grown a beard and had wood splinters in his fingers, but because he used clichés as a way of avoiding other people's pain.

One evening, leaning over the harbour wall, Keith watched a group of fishermen unload their catch. He recognised Conor's red hair. The other boy gave no sign of noticing him as he jumped onto the pier and wound a rope around a mooring post.

A dog dived from the pier, eagerly chasing a stick that had been flung into the water by his master, the old man Keith had met on the day of his arrival. Barney joined him, resting his elbows on the wall. "This your first time in our neck of the woods?" he asked.

"Yeah. And probably my last," Keith replied.

"Too many cuckoos in the same nest. That's the problem." He glanced quizzingly at Keith. "A funny old world, wouldn't you say?"

"Hilarious," said Keith. "How do you know so much about it?"

"That young lad over there gives me a hand sometimes when I do the fishing trips. Have you ever done any sea fishing yourself?"

"No. Catching mackerel has never been top of my fun list."

"Not that kind of fishing. Deep sea fishing." He bent to pick up the stick which the dog had retrieved and flung it outwards again. "I've promised to bring him out on the boat before I lay her up for the winter."

"Could I go?"

"Can't see any reason why not. That young lad needs a friend his own age. Not old codgers like me for company."

The boys walked back to the cottage together. For once Conor was in a talkative mood, boasting about the fish he had caught with Barney. Dog-fish and pollack and cod and conger eels so big they could strangle a whale.

"Some aquarium you have," scoffed Keith. "Full of dead fish."

Conor laughed. "That aquarium was just kids' stuff. This is the real thing."

"We won't stay out long," said Barney when they arrived at the pier the following morning. "The forecast is fair but it doesn't do to play with the tide this time of year."

When the boat was anchored out from shore it moved sluggishly in a constant see-sawing motion. Keith's mouth filled with saliva and he closed his eyes against the grey swell of water. Conor strode confidently around the deck, explaining about the break and strain of lines, when to strike and pump and reel. Mackerel were sliced as bait and attached to hooks.

Two hours passed without anything happening. Conor chewed a sandwich and poured tea from a flask. He offered a sandwich to Keith, who shook his head and huddled into himself, shivering, miserable. His stomach heaved and he was violently sick over the side of the boat.

"This is a dead loss," moaned Conor. "Nothing's biting."

"Give it time," said Barney. "It'll happen."

Even as he spoke, Conor's rod bent until Keith thought it would snap in two. The sea broiled and a fish appeared, exploding into mid-air, leaping, arching, writhing, desperately flinging its body away from the light. Keith stood rigid, watching each frantic movement the fish made as it landed on the deck.

"It's a pollack," Conor yelled. He held the twisting body with deft hands and reached for a wooden mallet.

"No need for that," said the old man. "You can throw him back after you weigh him."

"You must be joking. I have a freezer to stock." Conor brought the mallet firmly down on the pollack's head. The tail flashed in a last convulsion and the body was still. He moved to the other side of the boat and caught two conger eels, dealing with each one in the same efficient way.

"Ten more minutes, lads," Barney said. "Then it's time to pull anchor."

Keith felt a lurch on the end of his line. A tingling feeling ran along his arms as he lifted his rod and the line tugged again.

"You've got a bite!" Conor yelled. He called instructions, leaning so far over the side of the boat that Keith thought he would fall into the sea.

The strength of the fish amazed him. Muscles strained on his arms. His legs were braced tightly against the side. Sweat dripped into his eyes. He would never be able to haul this monstrous weight aboard. "There he is!" Barney lifted his hands in the air and shook his fists. "He's pulling hard but you've got him."

At first Keith thought it was a silver shadow on the water as the fish came into view. A last heave and it was landed. Tail thumping furiously, it slithered along the wooden slats.

Barney removed the hook from its mouth. "He's a big one. The biggest yet. Take him, son. He's all yours."

Keith tried to hold the fish but it thrashed in a frantic effort to escape. He grasped the slippery scales between his hands. But not deftly as Conor had done and the fish was free, wriggling crazily across the deck.

"Go . . . go . . . go!" Conor slapped his fingers against his mouth in a war whoop. "Go on. Finish him off. Kill him." He held out the mallet, challenging Keith, his face red and sharp from the wind that slapped the side of the boat.

"Leave me alone," Keith roared and dropped on all fours, trapping the fish between his knees.

The fish shuddered. It seemed to be drowning in air as Keith lifted the mallet above its head. His heart thumped, harder than the thudding fury of the fish. He wanted to smash it again and again until it lay in a pool of blood and glistening flesh. Only it was no longer the fish he saw but his father's head . . . and the mallet swinging downwards again and again . . . the sound like the splinter of breaking glass . . . the sound of everything in his life falling apart and coming together again in shapes that made no sense . . . yet they formed his future . . . and the future of the boy beside him who was laughing so hard that tears ran down his cheeks. Blood streaked the silver flesh. Keith realised his hands were bleeding, cut from the line that had hauled the fish aboard.

"Let it go, son," said Barney. "It's time to let it go."

With a shuddering cry Keith stood up and flung the fish overboard. It swerved crazily, stunned and lost in its familiar milieu, then plunged downwards. Foam gathered above the spot where it had disappeared and the water folded over again. Soon, not even a ripple marked its downward rush.

"Some hero you are," Conor made no attempt to hide his scorn. "What the hell did you go and do that for? You could have set a record with that weight."

Keith imagined the stillness beneath the waves. The silver fish blending into the murky shadows. He thought about the baby forming in Marianne's womb. Webbed fingers and toes, watery eyes opening to a new life in the summer. He thought about feelings. How they twined love and rage and pain and loss and guilt into a skein that he could no longer separate.

"He's probably dead," muttered Conor. His shoulders slumped and he sat down abruptly on the wooden bench. "Dead at the bottom of the sea. Fish food."

"He's not dead," said Keith. "He's back where he belongs."

"You're breaking my heart." Conor shoved his catch aside with his boot and unwrapped another sandwich. "He was only a fucking fish."

"Time we were going home, lads," Barney shouted.

The two boys turned their faces to the sea. Neither spoke as the boat headed towards the harbour.

THE NIGHT I FELT THE EARTH MOVE

Margrit Cruickshank

The first woman I ever slept with was called Marina. She was blonde, she was Swedish, she was a babe.

We were on this bonding course in Transition Year, getting to know each other better, discovering truths about ourselves (who wants to?) and each other (ditto in spades) in a Gulag in darkest Culchieland. You know the sort of thing: cell blocks with bunks and wooden floors. Primitive wasn't in it. There was even a perimeter fence; but they'd drawn the line at guard towers and machine gun emplacements. We were hardly going to escape, were we? The nearest bus stop was over two miles away.

Anyhow, the idea was that we'd go for long character-building hikes up perpendicular mountains, abseil down vertical cliffs, practise drowning in canoes, that sort of thing. Oh, and did I mention, this was all in April, i.e. a typical Irish spring? Sub-zero temperatures, gale-force winds, rain, mist – you name it, we had it.

Known as clean, healthy fun. Yes.

It was our fourth night there. I was supposed to be helping wash our lot's greasy dishes, it being my evening on the roster. But there was this group of women hikers at the other sink in the kitchen and the sight of their long tanned legs and short *short* shorts as they bent over the stainless steel basin (maybe, after Scandinavia, the Gulag didn't feel cold to them) interfered with my sense of direction. Like

45

magnetism interferes with a compass. I abandoned Julie and Ciaran and offered the services of my dishmop.

It turned out they were on a cycling holiday round Ireland. They were big into the scenery, they'd expected bad weather so weren't too fazed by the rain, and they were finding the locals very helpful. Their names were Marina, Brigitte and Anna. All this was told me as they leant against the draining board, wiping the odd plate, while I plunged elbow-deep in soapy water, showing just how helpful locals could be.

They came and sat with us in the common room afterwards and the *craic,* as they say, was mighty. Nice girls like Julie Kelly and her crowd were, well, nice to them while Nuala, Samantha and Clare gave them the deep freeze treatment and tried to make out us lads were their very own private property.

As if.

Around midnight, when most of our gang, worn out by another day of torture-masquerading-as-health, had headed for the sack (and our jailers, O'Keefe and Traynor, had vanished in their car, no doubt to the nearest pub), I suggested a walk up the valley in the moonlight. Yes, for once fate was smiling on me: the rain had stopped and the moon was doing its thing out of a clear starry sky. Everybody knows there's nothing like a bit of moonlight for romance.

Seven of us started out: me, Darren, Paul, the three Swedish girls – and Nuala. She was like that, Nuala; always sticking her nose in where it wasn't wanted.

Marina was the one I decided to go for. She had a figure that'd sell fish-net tights to old-age pensioners and this incredible, amazing, long blond hair. As we walked up the road away from the adventure centre, I waited for an opportunity to get her all to myself.

The valley looked different at night. The hills were much

more threatening than they'd seemed in the daytime and the moonlight spread totally black shadows under pine trees and behind stone walls. It was spooky. Exciting, but definitely spooky. I mean, I'm often out late at night in town but it's nothing like this was. There's *things* in town: cars, buildings, people. I don't think I could hack all this emptiness for long.

I walked close to Marina. Nuala walked close to me. Darren and Paul paired up with Brigitte and Anna – they'd known Nuala for long enough not to want to have anything to do with her.

So had I, for that matter. But Nuala could be like used chewing gum – impossible to scrape off. Especially when she had decided to latch on to someone. She wasn't bad-looking, Nuala. Just too available. Everyone in our year boasted they'd shagged her, but maybe it was all words. She'd obviously decided to target me this evening, possibly because she realised I'd got the hots for Marina. That would get right up Nuala's nose, ignoring her for some foreign piece.

The others were laughing and joking, but I was only half-concentrating. I was trying to work out whether to take Marina's hand now, or wait for a bit. The sooner the better, obviously, if I was going to get anywhere tonight. But I didn't want to move too fast and scare her off.

I walked more slowly and we started to fall behind. This was better. Now what, though? I could hardly just grab Marina's arm and drag her behind a wall. What we needed was lessons on how to score with the opposite sex, not a week of poxy open-air pursuits.

I let my hand brush against hers. She didn't say anything but she didn't move away either. Then we both spoke at once:

"What . . . ?"

"Where . . . ?"

"You go first."

"No, you go first."

"You. You're the visitor."

"I was going to ask where you think we should go tomorrow, Shane. What would be a nice route?"

It was like being doused with a bucket of cold water. Here was I, thinking all sorts of romantic thoughts – and she was planning their next day's itinerary! Still, I might turn it to some use . . .

"You could get the train up to Dublin and see the city. We're going back in a couple of days ourselves." *Only two more days in Culchieland – I might just make it!* "I'll give you my number and we can meet up and I'll show you round."

"I do not know. We like your Irish countryside."

"Dublin's a must," I argued. "There's a real buzz to it. Not as much as Copenhagen, maybe, but you'd be surprised."

"Copenhagen?"

Ooops! I thought quickly – geography was never one of my best subjects. "Don't you know Copenhagen? It's great. But then, so's . . . Oslo? And, er, Stockholm?" Stockholm! That was it!

"We are not from Stockholm. We come from a small village. We do not like cities."

I couldn't believe it. How could anyone not like cities?

And then another thought struck me. Everyone knows that Swedish towns are full of sex and free drugs, but Swedish villages might be as bad as Ballydehob! "You do have mixed saunas, though?" I heard myself asking.

She smiled in the moonlight. "Why is it everyone asks us about saunas?"

"It's just that you Swedes have a reputation for being . . . er . . . less hung up than we are about . . . um . . . sex and things," I muttered.

"Hung up?" Was she laughing at me?

48

"You know what I mean. Bothered. Worried."

"Are you bothered and worried about sex, Shane?"

She was definitely taking the piss. I upped the pace to catch up with Darren and the rest. The night was a wash-out. We might as well go home.

They were waiting for us in a car park at the top of the valley. Someone had obviously said something funny and they were laughing away like drains. At least somebody was enjoying the evening.

Paul handed round the smokes. Nuala took one, the three Swedish girls refused. We sat on the wall of the carpark and looked back down the valley. Then: "I'm heading back," Paul said. He turned to Anna. "Coming?"

And so we were five.

Darren was the next to make a move. He threw away his butt. "Paul's right. It's frigging cold out here."

That left three. Which, as everyone except Nuala knows, is a crowd.

My luck changed. Something – something big – breathed loudly behind a stone wall. Nuala jumped. "What's that?"

"It is a cow, stupid," Marina told her.

I hoped she hadn't noticed me jumping too.

"Go back if you're scared, why don't you?" I told Nuala.

"Are you coming with me?"

The moon disappeared behind a cloud. It was like a curtain came down: pitch black. The cow – or whatever it was – snorted loudly again. That finally did it for Nuala. Dropping my arm, she streaked off down the road after the others.

So, there I was with the girl of my dreams, all alone in the darkness. At last!

I moved closer to Marina. She moved away. The moon came out again.

Typical.

"We shall climb to the top of the hill?" Marina suggested. "Look, there is a path."

What? I looked up at the mountain: it was huge! She had to be insane. "Why don't we just stay here and . . . er, talk?" I asked.

"Come on, Shane. Do not be lazy. It is not far."

Not far? Who was she kidding?

On the other hand, she wanted to go off alone with me. Had I missed a signal here? I began to hope again. So, when she strode off up the path, I followed her.

Even though she'd changed her shorts for jeans before she came out, the way her bottom moved was . . . *Jeez!* I began to panic. What was I letting myself in for? She *must* have the same thing on her mind as I had. Why else would she be up here with just the two of us? She'd probably had loads of men already, she was Swedish after all – *would she guess that this was my first time?*

The night wasn't warm and yet I found myself sweating.

She bombed up the narrow path like Superwoman on speed. I soon found myself too out of breath trying to keep up with her to worry about what was going to happen when we stopped. At this rate, I remember thinking as my legs threatened to collapse under me, my heart banged in my chest and I gasped for air, I was heading for a heart attack rather than a first fantastic night of sex.

Marina finally paused to let me catch up. She pointed to the ridge ahead of us. "We will go to the top? It is good to reach the top."

I waited for my heart to stop pounding and for my breath to come back. "That won't be it," I told her. "You don't know these hills. They go on for ever. Any time you think you've reached the top it's just another frigging shoulder."

"I am sure it is the top. Come on, Shane. It would be a shame to turn back when we are so near."

What was I supposed to say? That I didn't give a monkey's about the mountain? That I'd only suggested a walk that evening so as to get her to . . . *You know.* I don't have to spell it out.

Maybe it was time to be masterful? "Tell you what. Let's just rest for a while and look at the view. Here," I pointed to a convenient rock. "Sit down for a minute."

"OK." She smiled and sat down. I did likewise. I had to perch on a sharp ridge of stone to get close to her, but that was OK: there were more important things on my mind.

"It's pretty chilly, isn't it?" I asked, rubbing my hands. I put an arm round her. "That better?"

She didn't exactly snuggle up to me, but she didn't shove me off, either.

I moved my head closer to hers. She smelt nice.

"Look!" she said. "You can see the adventure centre from here."

I opened my eyes again. Sure enough, there it was, nestling in its little hollow way down below us in the valley. The moon was silvering its roof and the river gleamed like tinsel between black trees. It was a very long way away. I tried not to think about the walk back.

I gave her a squeeze. This would have been a lot easier in summer, I found myself thinking. She was wearing a thick suede jacket over a jumper and jeans – and goodness knows what she had on underneath that. *You're going to find out, Shaney boy,* I encouraged myself. I decided to start with a kiss and take it from there.

Carefully, trying to keep my nose out of the way, I leant across her, aiming for her mouth.

She turned her head ever so slightly – so that my kiss landed on her cheek.

"Brrr." She shook herself. "You are right, Shane. It is cold. I think we should go home."

What the hell was she playing at?

Maybe, I tried to convince myself, she was making sure I didn't think she was too easy. Maybe this was just an opening move in the Swedish mating game.

I moved my lips in again.

Instead of the moist smoothness of her mouth, I found myself kissing the rough suede of her jacket as she stood up.

She *did* know what was going on, I realised angrily. She had got to her feet, just at that moment, quite intentionally. She'd been leading me on just so's she could humiliate me as soon as I made my move. She'd probably been laughing at me all along, probably only suggested climbing the bloody mountain just to make a fool of me. She must think me a total wuss. The bitch! Well, feck her!

Trying to pretend I'd only stumbled against her by mistake, I got up too. "OK. Come on, then."

The valley was *miles* away.

Forgetting everything we'd been told all week about safety, about how going downhill is more dangerous than going up, about not putting your foot in a hole and breaking your ankle, I ploughed down through the heather. Let *her* keep up with *me* this time, I thought. She's dragged me up her on false pretences. She never had any intention of even snogging me. She can bloody well find her own way down if she can't keep up.

The moon, sensing my mood, went into a sulk as well and disappeared behind a huge bank of clouds.

And that was when it happened.

I suddenly stepped into nothing. You know the way when you're going down stairs and you take a step that isn't there and your whole body goes into a state of shock? Well, it was like that to the power of four hundred. Suddenly the heather gave way and my foot went down into nothing. A black hole. Before I had time to realise what had happened – although not before I had time to scream like a two-year-old, which must have impressed Marina no end – I was tumbling down a cliff and crashing to a halt on a rock at the bottom. (OK, so "cliff" is probably a bit of an exaggeration, but it was bad enough. You should have been there.)

I actually heard something in my leg go *snap*. I mean, you read about that but you don't believe it. Marina slid down the heather to join me. It was pitch black now, as I said, and she was just a dark shadow. "Are you OK?"

What a typical stupid female remark! If I'd been OK I wouldn't have been lying there on my back, would I?

"Yeah," I groaned, as bravely as I could. "I've done something to my leg, though."

"Here. Hold my hand."

At last! Only like all the things that happen in my life, it came too late. I grabbed her hand, she tugged, I screeched again.

"Come on, Shane. You must try. We cannot stay here – it is too cold."

I tried. But as soon as I put any weight on my right leg, the pain hit me, *ker-pow*!

Marina squatted down beside me. "Are you sure you cannot make it? Even if you lean on me and we walk very slowly?"

I tried again. I was sure.

She hesitated. "I could go for help," she said. "But it is so dark and I could get lost or maybe hurt myself too. We were stupid to come so far."

She could say that again.

"The others will know which way we went. I think we should stay here until they find us."

Which is what we did.

She snuggled up to me (again, *at last*), wrapping herself around me and holding me against her chest. I could feel her boobs even through *both* our layers of clothes but neither of us was in the mood for snogging. It was far too cold for a start – even though I'd fallen down into a sort of sheltered hollow.

I must have passed out with the pain because the next thing I remember is this guy from the adventure centre, a couple of his mates and O'Keefe, our teacher, humping me like a sack of potatoes on to a stretcher and bumping me down the mountain back to civilisation, warmth, a doctor and a whole load of grief.

The adults were bad enough. "How could you be so stupid? What were you doing up there? Don't you realise the trouble you've caused?" That sort of thing.

But my mates were worse. "OK, you jammy bastard. Was it worth it?" they asked when I was brought back from the local hospital the next day, my leg in plaster. "What happened up there? Did you score?"

I grinned at them in triumph. "*Did I score?* You bet I did!"

The jealousy in their eyes was good to see.

"Yeah," I told them, trying to look suitably modest. "And, d'you know something? It's even better than they say it is! It's deadly! In fact – and you're not going to believe this – I actually felt the earth move!"

TAKING PICTURES

Rose Doyle

The rain began soon after the DART left Raheny. By the time it got to Sandymount the shower was falling steadily all across Dublin Bay. A thin, fair boy carrying a camera watched as it darkened and blotted the landscape and cursed with a silent, controlled ferocity. Another person might have yelled and kicked, given honest vent to anger at the way the elements were conspiring against him. The boy wasn't that kind of person. He considered himself pretty controlled, all things considered and given the way life had been getting at him lately. His parents had been known to disagree on this aspect of his character and so had some of his teachers. But they weren't living his life so they didn't understand a thing. Not one damn thing.

They didn't understand how *bored* he was, how much he wanted to be grown and gone and free of them all. If it hadn't been for the Canon EOS 50E he'd be a total basket case. Taking pictures of things as he saw them, freezing images as they grabbed him, gave a sort of purpose to his life. It was the only thing that did and was the reason he was on the DART today. He was on his way to get some very special pictures. Or had been, until the rain started.

The rain coming down and ruining the light was typical of the way his life had been going lately. Part of it he blamed on his age. Fifteen was a lousy, nowhere age to be.

You were expected to behave like an adult while being treated like a child. It was a loser's time of life. All of his friends were losers. They had to be, to bother being friends with him. He himself was a *numero uno* loser. No argument.

It looked like being a lifelong condition too. Only a long-term loser could have reached fifteen years of age without ever, once, having kissed a girl. Or being kissed by a girl. Without ever touching a girl or feeling one, anywhere. An arm or a neck or a shoulder would do to begin with. If you were to believe even the dopiest of his friends, girls were forever offering them the forbidden, terrifying parts of their bodies. He'd never been given a hint or a whisper. Definitely a loser.

He cleared his steamy breaths from the window and studied the quality and darkness of the rain. It was falling everywhere now, on the land as well as the sea. The bright, hopeful day that had urged him on to the train at Sutton might have been last week instead of just twenty minutes ago. There wasn't a snowball's chance of him getting decent pictures when he got to the Temple. With the sleeve of his sweatshirt he cleaned the window again. He would have worn a jacket if his mother hadn't started going on at him about it.

"It's going to rain," she'd yelled as he left the house.

Wishing she would stay out of his head he'd ignored her. Now the camera would get wet.

The rain was pelting, urged along by gusts of irritable wind, when he got off the train at Blackrock. The distance he'd put between himself and home made him feel a bit better. From here he could observe, but be untouched by, the area in which he lived. He liked the feeling of being cut off from all that went on there, from this parents, loser friends, infantile sister, crap school. But more than any of that he liked being in the vicinity of the Temple.

Trudging along it occurred to him that the rain might not be such a disaster after all. It would keep people away, give him the Temple to himself, alone, for the whole of this scabby, wet afternoon. Only a crazy loser would go crawling around its stones and lichen in the rain. Only someone like him. The rain dripped from his nose. To protect the Canon he hung it under his sweatshirt. It was unlikely he'd get even half-decent pictures. There was neither light nor visibility. He hoped the rocks wouldn't be too slippery. He didn't want to fall with the camera.

He began to trot when the pillars and broken walls of the old building came into view. It was like a magnet, the way it fascinated him, filling him with curiosity and a sense of its mystery, from the very first time he'd spotted it on its rocky perch.

He'd been on the DART that day too and had hopped off at Seapoint to make his way back to suss it out. He hadn't been able to decide what exactly the building was supposed to be, even as he stood in its circular shade and peered at the sea through its openings. It seemed to him like a Temple but was probably a Victorian folly of some sort, or an old changing room, or summer house. It didn't much matter and he didn't much care. He liked it, whatever it was, and he liked being inside it. Not knowing meant it could be anything in his imagination. He decided it would be a Temple.

That first time had been months before, in the summertime, and he'd sworn to himself then that he would be back to take pictures.

He reached the rocks and cautiously, holding the Canon tightly against his chest, began to make his way over them to the Temple. Today it seemed to him an outpost, more of a stony grey fortress over the bay. If he managed to get pictures he intended making them into a montage that he could hang on the wall of his room. With a bit of luck the sun might come out again. And pigs might fly, an event just as likely, given his luck.

He was soaked to the skin by the time he got to the shelter of the Temple. Shivering, he sat against a wall and took the camera from beneath his sweatshirt. He focused through the gap in the wall opposite and got a spectacular grey blur. Feeling the ground wet under him, he stood up, looking for a drier spot.

When he found one he hunkered down, careful not to put his bum on the ground this time, and willed the rain to ease, even a little. It did, suddenly and within minutes. Hardly believing his luck he blinked, lifted the camera to his eye and focused on the large drops dripping from the jagged edges around the Temple entrance.

He thought the head was piece of rock when it first appeared in the lens. When it moved he went very still and zoomed in, holding the camera on its strange motion and studying it until it became clear to him that it was a human head and that its owner was a girl who was rocking herself to and fro.

"Head banger," he muttered, but not too loud. Her black hair was streaming wet and what he could see of her face was very white. She looked to be about his age but in the circumstances he couldn't be sure. As he watched she put a hand to her head and brushed her hair back. It was a long hand, thin and elegant. He snapped a quick shot.

"Do you make a practice of spying on people and taking their picture?" The girl's angry face turned on him in the lens. It was a lovely, lovely face, even when distorted by anger and red-eyed from crying. For the second time in minutes he blinked. Then he put the camera down.

"Sorry." He stood up. "It just happened."

"Did it, indeed?" Her voice was tart and a bit hoarse. She looked away from him and hugged her knees to her chest. She was wearing jeans and a T-shirt.

Like him she had no jacket and like him she was soaked through. He took a step towards her. "Leave me alone, will you . . . ?" She didn't turn or look at him. He supposed she sensed his movement. "I'll scrap the picture, if it upsets you so much," he said, but he was lying. She was so very beautiful. He'd never been so close to anyone as gorgeous as she was. Even her hand and the side of her face were beautiful. He would build the Temple montage around her picture.

"Don't bother, if it upsets *you* so much," she said and he wondered again at her intuitive sense. Maybe she was a witch of some kind. Or maybe she was just in tune with the elements and her senses. He risked a couple more steps in her direction and this time she said nothing. When he was within touching distance she stood up.

"Do you always do what it suits you to do?"

As a question it was a statement. Not that he could have answered her anyway. Her green eyes, levelled on his, had taken his breath away. She was so perfect she was unreal, a dream. Every dream he'd ever had, in fact. He stared, stupidly. She was about his own age, maybe a little older. Her hair, like a black frame around her small face, made him want to take her picture again. He didn't dare. Just as he didn't dare give in to the urge to touch her.

"You some sort of retard, or something?" The tiredness in her voice belied the harsh words. She looked away with an infinitely weary shrug which left her shoulders hunched and spoke again. "I didn't think there'd be anyone here. I don't suppose you did either."

"No. No, I didn't." His voice sounded all right when eventually it came out. Not squeaky anyway. "I came to take pictures. I hadn't counted on the rain." He indicated the camera, his eyes still fixed on her averted face. "I like this place." He could hear his voice grow uncertain as he went on, "I call it the Temple, to myself that is. It seems to me a place where anything could have happened. Could happen. Human sacrifices. Anything . . . " She was looking at him again and he stumbled to a muttering stop. Her eyebrows were lifted in dark surprise.

"God, you're a child," she said, "but still, I know what you mean. I often think things like that myself about this place. The shape of it and the stones and where it is . . . and its loneliness . . . " She stopped with another small shrug and lifted her face to his with a sad smile. "You think I'm mad now, I suppose, a crazy who sits in the rain and talks about stones being lonely . . . ". She made no reference to her crying but he knew that she knew he knew. Clearly it was something she wanted to pretend hadn't happened.

"I don't think you're a crazy," he said. What he thought was that she was out of this world, a vision, and that he was the one who was crazy. Crazy if he didn't do something about getting to know her.

"Do you live near here?" he asked.

"Not far away." She was quiet, looking past him at the houses of Blackrock. He was again aware of the sadness in her face. He wanted to ask her about it but before he could find any words she spoke again.

"Rain's stopped," she said. "I'd better be going . . . "

"Don't. I want to take your picture." They weren't the words he wanted and they came out before he could stop them. The camera felt a ton weight round his neck and he wondered how long he could hold his breath while he waited for her to answer. She took forever.

"You've got your nerve," she sniffed at last. "You've already taken my picture without asking . . . " She paused and he had a real feeling that she was secretly pleased he'd asked her. He relaxed. "OK," she said and looked around the Temple, "where to you want me to stand?"

In the next half hour he came closer to happy than he'd

been for a long, long time. They talked while he snapped, about music at first, but about photography too when she asked him why he was so keen. He told her why, almost understanding himself and why he took pictures by the time he'd finished.

"It puts a shape on what I see," he said, "sort of focuses the world for me. I feel in control of things while I'm taking pictures, like I'm making something happen."

"You are," she said, "making something happen, I mean."

"I am?"

The way she was smiling at him did wild things to his heart and stomach. He wanted to freeze the moment, in all its wonder and colours, and frame it where he would be able to see and study it forever. Instead, he stared at her stupidly until she shook her head and poked him in the chest with a finger.

"You're making a studio of this old temple," she said, "and we're having a laugh."

As if to make the point she shook the hair from her face, gave a short bark and struck a pose. When he went back to taking her picture the sadness wasn't so deeply in her face as it had been before. But she still seemed to him unreal, a beautiful creature from another dimension, or one at least beyond his knowing. She was a natural model too, positioning herself exactly where he said, smiling, scowling, pulling crazy faces as the mood took her. She was cool, unselfconscious in a way that was adult. Loading the camera with a second roll of film he wondered if she'd posed before, if maybe she was a model. But when he asked her she laughed.

"No way," her voice was light and she looked out to sea. "Thought once I'd have a go at it all right . . . " She gave her familiar shrug and he resisted another lunatic urge to put his arm around her. "No way I could do it now anyway. I've fucked up too much for anything like that."

They were close to one another, about three feet apart. He'd been trying for her profile against the Temple opening. She turned to him as she finished speaking, her eyes filled with tears.

His hand moved without him telling it and he caught a tear with his finger as it fell.

"Don't," he said, "please don't be sad."

She became very still as she stared up at him, quiet as the stones around them and just as frozen looking. He felt like a man beside her, she was so slight and childlike. But her eyes, years and years too old, made him unsure again. There was nothing of childhood, or even of youth, in the way they were looking at him. They were a woman's eyes, full of knowledge and of the weary sadness he'd seen in her already.

"You're a nice . . . " She paused and put a hand to his face and he thought dimly that if she said the word "boy" he would die on the spot. Her hand felt soft, and surprisingly warm, and the word she said, before moving her hand to the back of his neck and gently pulling his face down to hers, was "person".

As a first kiss it was everything. It was the sea and sun and the sound of the gulls circling overhead. It was warm and it was cold and had a small breeze in it as well as the salt from the tears drying on her face. He could taste salt on her lips too when they met his, their soft pressure terrifying him before he found the courage of need and drew her gently to him to kiss her properly.

"Get your fuckin' hands off her."

The words hit him at precisely the moment their owner's fist caught him on the shoulder. When he spun away from the girl the same fist caught him on the side of the jaw.

He wheeled, shocked and caught off guard, across the Temple to fall on a couple of stone slabs. He was trying to get up, to focus on the girl while wondering where he'd dropped the camera, when a boot caught him in the stomach and sent him sprawling backwards on to the slabs again. Winded, aware of dull pain everywhere, he tried once more to get up. He knew that if he could get on his feet he'd be able to deal with the creep, whoever he was. He could hear the girl yelling something, her voice high and shrill. The boot thudded into his chest again and as he fell to his knees its owner's voice, hateful and gloating, echoed about the Temple.

"Stay away from her, you little shit, do you hear me? Stay away from her and stay away from this place too, you hear?"

The boy saw him now, hulking and handsome and wearing a black leather jacket. He looked old, about twenty or so. The boot lashed at him again, with less force this time, as the girl caught and pulled at the jacket. She held on to his arm when he leaned down and began to talk to the boy.

"Listen, turd face." His breath smelled of alcohol. The boy met his gaze but didn't try to get up. "I'm letting you off easy 'cos you're only a kid. The next time I won't be so forgiving and you won't be so lucky. Only there won't be a next time, will there?" Expecting an answer to this he stopped and fixed the boy with a black glare. When the boy said nothing the man caught the front of his sweatshirt and pulled him so close the boy could see where he'd missed a few black hairs shaving.

"There won't be a next time because if there is I'll fuckin' kill you, do I make myself clear?"

Staring, the boy still said nothing. It wasn't that he was particularly brave. More that he was afraid how his voice would sound and didn't want to let himself down in front of the girl. The man's voice was confident, full of a soft, dead menace when next he spoke.

"The woman you were crawling all over is the mother of my child," he said, "she doesn't want you near her. I don't want you near her. Don't come back." He let go of Barry's jumper and dropped him back onto the slabs. His back hurt and it was several seconds before he twisted to look up at the man again. He had a grin on his face and he was holding the Canon.

"Nice little item you got here," he said, "get it from Santa Claus, did you?"

"Leave my camera alone." The second he yelled the boy knew he'd made a terrible mistake.

"Well, now," the man opened the back of the camera and removed the roll of film, "since you saw fit to help yourself to what is mine I think I'm entitled to what's yours . . . " He tossed the film over his shoulder and Barry heard it hit a rock and knew it had gone into the sea.

"And now, sonny boy," the man dangled the camera by its strap, "take a last look at your toy." He swung the Canon in a wide arc and let go. It sailed unerringly through the opening after the film. The boy was in no doubt that it too had landed in the sea.

The man and woman walked away without another word. The woman didn't once look back at the boy, not even when they came to the point where they disappeared from view. She seemed to belong by the man's side, to be old and of the world and not remotely like someone he could ever have kissed. Or who could have kissed him.

He felt in his pocket for the first roll of film. It was still there. He would have the pictures, at least. Frozen images of his fantasy woman.

I WANT TO HOLD YOUR HAND

Soinbhe Lally

The Milk Bar was the place to be that term. Eileen wouldn't have known something like that only that Theresa went every day after school and where Theresa went, Eileen followed. Convent girls sat in the corner near the jukebox. It gave Theresa the opportunity to make comments whenever someone from another school came to pick a song.

Theresa wore her hair in a long fringe which hung right down to her thick-lensed glasses. When she talked she waved her cigarette about, showing off her nicotine-stained fingers. She'd snogged enough fellows to be able to compare their kissing styles. Eileen longed to have long straight hair and nicotine-stained fingers. Her hair was short and curly. The one time she tried smoking it made her sick.

Between the convent girls and the big window which looked into the street sat the seminary boys. They didn't have uniforms. They were expected to dress like gentlemen, which meant that they all dressed like their fathers, in tweed sports jackets. They could have dressed with style. For example, they might have worn corduroy jackets with leather elbow patches, like their tall lean French teacher who was big into Beaudelaire and *fin de siècle* decadence, but they didn't.

Right opposite the seminary boys was the green corner. Green for Collegiate. Sem boys said Collegiate girls wore green uniform knickers too. Maybe. Boys were good liars.

You could never tell for sure whether a boy was telling the truth or just fantasising.

Collegiate girls made the most noise. They shrieked instead of giggling and talked in loud voices about free love and how many purple hearts it took to make you high. When any of them came to the jukebox they looked the convent girls over with their we're-too-cool-to-talk-to-you look and then turned their backs.

Convent girls wore navy. Navy for naive. Theresa said the nuns were to blame. They even cut the chapter on reproduction out of the O-level biology book. "They'll never ask you about that in the exam, so it doesn't matter," said Sister Mary Claire.

"That's not much use to us if somebody gets pregnant and doesn't know how it happened," Theresa said when Sister Mary Claire had left the room and everybody thrilled to hear her use an obscene word like "pregnant".

Eileen tried to compensate by being intellectual. She did the crosswords from yesterday's newspapers. She read Dickens. *A Tale of Two Cities* was her favourite. She saw the film with Dirk Bogarde and got a lump in her throat when Dirk Bogarde stood in the tumbrel saying, "It's a far far better thing I do than I have ever done."

About music, her feelings were mixed. Classical was very intellectual and all that but the trouble with classical composers was that they were all dead. You couldn't see them on TV with long hair and Beatle suits, like John Lennon and Paul McCartney. Theresa was wild about the Beatles. "I'd snog any of them any night," she said when she pinned their pictures to the classroom notice-board. Eileen was more discriminating. She liked John Lennon. The composer John Lennon.

Right opposite, beside the Milk Bar counter, were the black and yellow striped blazers of the other boys' school. They had straw boaters. Most of them wore them tilted over their eyes. It meant they had to hold their heads high to see in front of them, which made them look superior. Others carried their boaters languidly in their hands.

"Jaysis," Theresa said when any of them came to the jukebox, "I'd snog him, so I would."

When things changed, they changed abruptly. On a Thursday afternoon one of the black and yellow striped boys crossed the invisible line that divided the milk bar and sat on an empty stool right beside Eileen. He placed his straw boater in his lap. Eileen stopped mid-clue and stared. Theresa fell silent and sucked dramatically on her cigarette.

"Are any of you girls interested in politics?"

Nobody answered. What kind of question was that? Politics were something you were born to, predestined to belong to one side or the other. Being interested had nothing to do with it.

The boy didn't wait for a reply. "My name's Wesley. Our English teacher, Mr Jones, asked me to tell you that there will be an inaugural meeting to form a young Liberal association tomorrow night, in the Imperial Hotel. We'd like it if you'd come along." He handed out typed notices.

"I bet you're a Methodist," Theresa said. She waved her cigarette and wafted smoke all over him.

The boy blushed. "Yes. Actually I am."

"I've never heard of anyone called Wesley who wasn't a Methodist. You Methodists get called Wesley just like our fellows get called Pius. I have a brother called Pius."

"What do Liberals stand for?" Eileen asked.

"Principles. You know, things like abolishing capital punishment and joining the common market and Vietnam."

"Vietnam?" Theresa exhaled a cloud of smoke.

"It's Liberal policy that America should stay out of Vietnam."

"What about partition? Shouldn't the British stay out of Ireland?" she asked.

"That's the sort of issue we have to get away from,"

Wesley said. "The Liberal party rises above all that. We're concerned with real politics, not history."

He wore his brown hair long, nearly as long as John Lennon's. Eileen noticed how it kept falling over his eyes so that he had to shake it back now and again with a toss of his head. She would have liked to reach out and push it back for him.

"I want to hold your hand," the Beatles sang from the jukebox.

Eileen sipped her milk shake, glanced at her newspaper and pencilled in a word, hoping Wesley would notice that she was doing the cryptic crossword, not the easy one. When she turned to him again she tried to sound vague so that he wouldn't know how interested she was. "OK."

"See you tomorrow night so." Wesley rose and went to the next table.

"Why did you say you'd go?" Theresa asked.

"Because he's nice."

"What will your father say?"

"Who cares?"

They nearly didn't go. The maths teacher gave a load of extra homework to be done overnight and they wouldn't have had time only that each did one half of the work and then they copied from each other.

"Where are you going?" Eileen's mother asked.

"Sodality meeting." It would have been too complicated to explain.

The inaugural meeting was held in an upstairs room. Everyone was out of school uniform although pre-faded blue denims were practically a uniform, except that with denims everyone looked the same.

Theresa's brother Pius was there. He sat in front with a couple of pals. The lean seminary French teacher was there, wearing corduroy and looking decadent, probably thinking about Beaudelaire.

A small fat man with glasses introduced himself. Mr

Jones. He was Chairman of the Fermanagh Liberal association and he was also an English teacher. He spoke with a cultured, British voice. An election was forthcoming. Young Liberals were needed.

He explained that candidates for the committee would have to be nominated. Names were called out and quickly seconded. The *fin de siècle* French teacher sat at a table and wrote them down. "We need one more," said the English teacher. Eileen heard her name being called and seconded. Theresa nudged her hard, right in the stomach. By the time she recovered her breath she was a committee member of the West Ulster Young Liberal Association.

It was intoxicating. The flood tide of the future was sweeping them to a better world.

The meeting ended and the *fin de siècle* teacher heaped party leaflets into her arms. She went home alone. "I'll stay," Theresa said. "They're going down to the bar."

Eileen brought the leaflets to bed. They were printed on yellow paper because black and yellow were the Liberal party's colours. Like Wesley's school uniform. She checked her atlas to find out exactly where Vietnam was. A long way from America. "Americans out of Vietnam" she wrote in inflammatory red ink across the cover of her précis text book. That'll show them, she thought ardently.

"Jaysis," Theresa said next day, "I should have taken up politics long ago. It's full of men."

"Did you snog any of them?"

"Not yet, they were all dead serious last night talking about politics. I can wait."

Eileen's father read her name in the local paper. How was she to know that they would go putting her name in the paper? There was a list of the newly elected Young Liberal committee members, tucked below several inches of column about the candidate who was being sent from Liberal HQ in London.

"You're a disgrace to your family," her father said. "Your

grandfather will turn in his grave. And your great-grandfather and his father too."

"It's time to put history behind us. We're a new generation," Eileen retorted bravely.

Her father brought down a fist on the table and made the dinner plates tremble. "I little thought I'd bring up a daughter who would side with an Englishman against her own people."

"It's got nothing to do with being Irish or English. Liberals are above all that. Anyway, we'll all be Europeans when we get into the Common Market. English, Irish, French, Italian, there will be no difference between them."

"No difference?" her father roared. "Men died to make Ireland free and you're going about calling yourself a Liberal. Lloyd George was a Liberal. You know what he did for Ireland."

"Lloyd George is history."

"Eileen, will you listen to your father and stop talking about things you know nothing about?" her mother intervened.

"I know all about them."

"You know damn all." Her father brought down his fist a second time and the dinner dishes trembled again.

"Well then, if you know so much, tell me what's your policy on Americans in Vietnam?"

She had him there. He scowled and went back to eating his dinner. "Begod, your grandfather and your great-grandfather and his father too, they would turn in their graves," he muttered between mouthfuls of potato and cabbage.

Let them turn, Eileen thought defiantly. The past is history. The future is politics.

At the next meeting she told about her father's objections. Wesley looked at her with admiration shining in his eyes. A lock of hair kept falling over his forehead, making him look like John Lennon.

There was a change in seating arrangements in the Milk Bar. Young Liberals sat together in the jukebox corner. "I want to hold your hand," the Beatles sang, again and again and again.

Green, navy, tweed, yellow and black were together at the same table. They were a set. People who didn't belong gave envious glances. Eileen, when she noticed them at all, threw back an I'm-too-cool-to-talk-to-you look. Wesley sat beside her and held her hand. He talked passionately about Vietnam. From time to time he tossed his long hair out of his eyes and looked like John Lennon.

The first time he walked her home he stopped at the big sycamore by the river and asked, "Have you ever snogged?"

"No."

"Me neither."

"That's all right." She put out her hand and pushed his long hair back out of his eyes. "I've always wanted to do that," she said.

They stopped going to the Milk Bar because they had to write addresses on forty thousand envelopes. The English teacher's dining-room was converted into election HQ. His small plump wife fretted, fearful that anyone would lean too heavily and leave marks on her polished Hepplewhite reproduction dining table.

"Do be careful," she fussed. "Don't use biros, they penetrate."

Theresa's brother Pius sniggered at that. Eileen couldn't think why. She would ask Theresa later.

"We're the first political party to send manifestos to all of the voters in this constituency," said the *fin de siècle* French teacher proudly as he placed bundles of envelopes and electoral lists in front of each of them. "The other parties only send them to their own voters."

Theresa looked at him dreamily through thick lenses. "Jaysis, I could snog him," she sighed.

The manifesto carried a picture of the candidate. Eileen felt a vague disappointment. He looked so middle-aged. Why couldn't they have sent someone attractive?

Theresa examined him critically. "I wouldn't vote for him. I wouldn't even snog him. I hate moustaches. They're itchy."

"How do you know that moustaches are itchy?"

"They look itchy."

"Anyway, you don't have a vote."

"Yes I do."

"You're too young."

"I've been voting ever since my granny died. Ask Pius. She had the same name as me."

"Does Theresa vote, Pius?"

"Yeah. She's been voting for years."

Eileen turned back to Theresa. "How do you convince them that you're twenty-one?"

"I get a postal vote."

"Oh." Eileen pondered a moment. "Who will you vote for this time?"

"I haven't made up my mind."

The candidate telephoned to ask for a motorcade to escort him into town.

"Jaysis, who does he think he is, John F Kennedy?" Theresa said when she caught her first glimpse of him. The year before she had pinned a picture of the American President to the classroom notice-board and kissed it every day. Then he got assassinated and she pinned up the Beatles instead.

The candidate sat with his wife in the back seat of an open-topped car. Each of them wore an enormous yellow and black rosette. The motorcade straggled along behind. As a motorcade it was a failure. It got mixed up with other traffic along the way. By the time it reached the town it included a bread van, a tractor and an express bus which kept honking to get by.

The motorcade passed the war memorial, crossed the bridge and went up Townhall Street where it came to a halt in front of the Imperial Hotel. The candidate tried to speak a few words before going inside but the bus kept honking so nobody actually heard what he said.

It was several days before the Young Liberals met him. He came one evening while they were addressing envelopes. A TV camera followed him. The candidate sat down and wrote on an envelope while a cameraman stood on a Hepplewhite reproduction chair to get a better shot. The candidate left then, followed by the camera.

Eileen's father saw it on the six o'clock news. The cameraman on the Hepplewhite chair had done a close-up of her addressing envelopes. "Oh Lord," he moaned. "What would your grandfather say, or your great-grandfather, or his father before him? They'll turn in their graves, Lord help us, when they see that."

Two days before polling day the candidate announced his intention of canvassing Brookhill. "As a citizen of the British Commonwealth I consider myself free to go wherever the Queen's writ runs," he said with a determined air.

"Maybe over in London they think that people here are used to politics," Theresa said dubiously. Neither she nor Eileen had ever actually been in Brookhill. It was just another housing estate on the edge of the town but people knew where lines were drawn and kept to their own side of them. "Carry a handbag," Theresa's brother Pius advised, "with something heavy in it."

Eileen filled up a large cologne bottle with water. The cologne was nearly finished anyway. It made a reassuring weight in her mother's handbag which she borrowed without asking. It would be too complicated to explain.

The candidate led the way into the estate, stopping to shake hands with passers-by. He moved round the corner into the next street, followed by cameras. Eileen stayed behind to help Wesley and Pius paste election posters on to telegraph poles.

A burly man approached them. "What do you lot think you're doing?"

A second man appeared from a gateway. "We don't want no litter on our street." He pulled down a poster and threw it on the ground.

Pius didn't hesitate. He threw the paste over the first man and flung the bucket at the second. A third man appeared. Wesley lashed out with the paste brush. At the same instant Eileen swung wildly with her mother's handbag and heard a sound of breaking glass as the cologne bottle shattered. They took to their heels and raced round the corner. The cameras were waiting for them.

The candidate said he was shocked. He stood in front of the cameras and said several times how shocked he was. Next day party leaders in Britain condemned hooliganism and attacks on party workers. On the six o'clock news there was another close up of Eileen. Her father chuckled wickedly. "That's the stuff," he said with glee. "If only your grandfather was here to see it. And your great-grandfather and his father too."

Eileen spent ages drying out her mother's handbag and picking out fragments of glass. It reeked of cologne. Maybe she wouldn't notice.

The eve of election meeting was scheduled for eight o'clock in a square off the High Street. Meetings by other parties would follow. There were two platforms, one in the centre of the square and one in a corner behind High Street. At eight o'clock there was only a handful of supporters at the corner platform which was draped with yellow bunting. Two policemen stood at a discreet distance. The candidate spoke at length about the Common Market and Vietnam, especially about Vietnam. He was eloquent about Buddhist monks who doused themselves in gasoline just to prove a principle.

The hour wore on and the handful of listeners became a crowd. Quickly the crowd grew rowdy and became a mob. The candidate was heckled. He raised his voice defiantly but his voice was drowned by loud cheers. A green, white and orange flag was being raised on a flagpole on the other platform. Eileen noticed that there were more than two policemen now. At the High Street entrance to the square, peaks of policemen's caps, row upon row of them, shone under the street lights.

"Why isn't that flag on your platform?" a heckler shouted. The candidate's retort was drowned in the roar of the mob.

The crowd surged forward. "Get in here," Wesley said, ducking into the empty space under the platform and pulling Eileen in after him. Theresa followed. The crowd suddenly changed direction. It swept away from the corner and across the square towards the narrow streets at the other end. All at once everybody was running. Eileen peered out and saw policemen baton their way to the flag and pull it down. Their polished boots shone under the street lights.

"Well done," Wesley cheered.

"What do you mean, well done?" Theresa asked indignantly.

"Well, we have to have law and order, don't we? That flag's a provocative emblem."

"No it's not."

"Yes it is."

"It's not." She pulled her hand away from his.

"It is," he said defiantly.

"Come on away out of this," Theresa said. "I'm sick of politics."

"Me too," Eileen agreed. She felt her eyes grow wet. Her bottom lip quivered.

"What's wrong?" Wesley asked.

She sniffed and felt in her pocket for a handkerchief.

Could he not see it for himself? Could he not see that the great tide of the future which had washed over them was ebbing now, leaving nothing but history behind? She found her handkerchief and blew her nose. "We're not ready for politics, are we?" she said. "I mean, when you come right down to it, what has Vietnam got to do with us?"

"To hell with Vietnam," Wesley said bitterly. "That flag's a provocative emblem whether you like it or not."

"I don't think it is."

There was nothing more to say. They came out from under the platform. The crowd was gone, the square almost empty. Wesley didn't walk Eileen home. "I'll see you round," he said. She knew that he wouldn't. He walked away, tossing his hair out of his eyes as he went. Never had he looked more like John Lennon. How long does it take, she wondered, for a broken heart to mend?

She walked home with Theresa. Pius overtook them. "For a few minutes there, it was beautiful, wasn't it?" he said, his eyes shining. He put a protective arm round Eileen. She looked up at his profile under the street lamps. He looked a bit like Dirk Bogarde. It was odd that she had never noticed before. She could fancy Pius riding in a tumbrel doing a far far better thing than he had ever done.

She wondered if he ever snogged. Theresa might know. To hell with politics, she thought, as she put her handkerchief back in her pocket.

HONORARY MEMBER

Chris Lynch

They say that in there somewhere we're all a little of this and a little of that. Both sides of everything existing at the same time inside the same guy. Opposites add up to everything.

Like Pauly and me, right? We make no sense to anybody but ourselves. We are the wrong people for each other, nothing alike, but somehow we fill each other in. Pauly completes me, does the stuff I can't do, thinks the thoughts I'd never think, brings *action* to my life that I'd miss without him.

If it were not for Pauly I wouldn't know what it was like to dive into the quarry.

If it were not for Pauly I wouldn't know what a worm tastes like.

If it were not for Pauly I wouldn't know that I am smart. I know because he tells me and because he shows me that he is not.

So we do a sort of inverse thing for each other: he provides me with the whoosh that makes the drag-ass parts of living more worth it; and I provide him the vacuum of experience that allows him to still feel any whoosh at all.

If I ever get married, there's nobody but Pauly for best man.

However, if I ever kill a person, that person is also Pauly.

Valentine's Day.

Pauly's thinking. He's always thinking, but especially on holidays, he's thinking.

"You thinkin' what I'm thinkin'?" he asks me over the phone. "It's Saturday. It's Valentine's, and it's Saturday."

77

"Pauly, I'm never thinkin' what you're thinkin'. Nobody's ever thinkin' what you're thinkin'."

"OK," he concedes. "I'm thinkin' let's go work out."

"See what I mean?" I tell him. "How would I ever have guessed that, that Valentine's means working out?"

"Proves you don't know me," he says. He's serious, and he's disappointed. "Be ready in fifteen minutes."

I am ready in fifteen minutes. Pauly picks me up in forty, beeping the embarrassingly hick-sounding horn of his old red Ford pickup. There is somebody I don't know riding in the bed. I nod, he nods.

"Who's he and where are we going?" I ask when I'm inside and the rear wheels are kicking up gravel.

"Who's who?" Pauly asks.

I point out the small sliding window behind our heads. "Him. The person rolling all over the place in the back of your truck." And he is, he's flopping around madly, with the way Pauly drives. The guy tries to get himself a seat up on the wheel well, Pauly nails a frost heave, and the guy is sprawling again.

"Oh," Pauly says, turning around to see. "Shit if I don't know. I never seen him before."

"Lie," I say.

"No lie," he says. Which doesn't mean that he's not lying, but it doesn't mean that he is, either. It doesn't mean anything, is what it means.

"OK, so you don't know this guy. Is he going with us to work out?"

"I don't know. Better check." Pauly slides the little window. "You wanna go work out?"

"Ya," the guy says.

Pauly slides the window closed. "Nah, he's not going."

I don't bite. Pauly's in one of those moods. When he is, it's smartest not to bite.

"So where are we going to work out, Paul?"

"Really nice new club down in Blue Falls. My brother Henry told me about it."

"You don't have a brother Henry. You don't have a brother at all."

"Do so. I just don't mention him much because he's the family embarrassment."

"Lie."

"No lie."

The small window slides open. "I'm Leon," Leon says, sticking his hand into the cab for me to shake.

"Hey," I say and I go to shake his hand until Pauly accelerates. Leon and his hand get sucked backward out of view.

"Why'd ya do that?" I ask.

"Because I'm jealous," Pauly says. "You belong to me."

I do a whole-body shiver. "Cut it out, Pauly. You know it makes me nervous when you say that stuff."

"That's why I say it. Your anxiety is always such a rush to those of us around you."

"You're welcome," I say as we pull into the parking lot of the gym.

The place looks more like a country music club than a health spa. It's two turns off the main road, carved out of thick woods, in a nowhere section of a suburb of nowhere. The building is a large wooden barn-shaped structure with a great big front wall but only a little bitty front door with an even bittier neon sign above it that reads simply "The Club."

"Don't look like much, does it?" says Leon, coming up from behind as we stand sizing the place up.

"Well it's a lot of much," Pauly says. "And anyway, I thought you were headed somewhere?"

"Thanks for the lift," Leon says, but doesn't make like he's going anywhere.

So Pauly and I leave him there in the lot among the four other cars that were there ahead of us.

"You a member?" the front desk attendant asks Pauly. He's a big guy, but with those big buff shiny useless muscles you get from a health club.

"No, I'm not a member," Paul says. "But my friend here is."

I cut in before he gets us in trouble. You have to be always ready to do that with Pauly. "No," I say to the attendant. "I'm not a member. But I could be. If it's any good, I might become a member."

"Oh good," the guy says, as if he gives a damn whether or not I join. "Well then, you can try us out for free today as an honorary member."

"Cool," I say.

Pauly snorts a laugh. At me, or maybe at the guy.

"And you?" the attendant asks Paul. "You interested in becoming a member?"

"Hell, no," Pauly says.

"Five bucks," the guy says, putting two locker keys and two towels up on the counter, a black-and-white checked one for me, and a green one for Pauly.

I follow my friend through the door, down a short corridor past the men's toilet, past two curtained dressing rooms, into the main locker room. There are a few guys undressing at different locations, two sweaty ones who are on the way out, one dry one just arriving like us. As we pass one sweaty one Pauly nods and points.

"Nice hog, dude," he says.

"Thanks," the dude responds as if they were talking about his car.

I gasp. I try to speak to my friend, but only gasp again. When we do reach our lockers, I grab him by the back of the shirt. He's opening the locker, on his merry way.

"What?" he says to me. "What? Something wrong?"

"What kind of a milk dud are you?" I say. "You don't say that kind of thing to a guy. To a *naked* guy, in a locker of a men's gym."

"Well, duh, Oakley," he says to me and proceeds to put stuff in his locker. "I couldn't very well say it if he was dressed. If he had his clothes on, how would I know what his hog looked like?"

"Shhhh!" I whisper, urgently. I glance over my shoulder

to see if anybody caught that. They all did, since they are staring at us. "Would you stop saying that stuff. *Jeez*."

"Why?" Pauly wants to know.

"Don't play this shit with me, Pauly. I hate it when you play this."

"Play what?" He has now slithered out of the shirt while I am still clutching it. He's pulling down his jeans.

"Pretending you're stupid. You know you're not supposed to talk about it."

"About what? About a guy's hog?"

"*Jesus,* Pauly," I say.

"No, Oak, I really don't get it. Why can't we say nice hog? I mean, jeez, did you *see* the damn thing? *Somebody* ought to stand up and say something to the guy, if not applaud."

"No," I insist. "I did not see it."

"Lie," he says.

"No lie," I say.

"Then you ought to get yourself a guide dog, because that thing was a sapling and a half."

"Never mind," I say. "The point is, you're not supposed to notice – even if you do. And nobody talks about it. I don't care if he's got one growing out of his damn forehead, you just say nice hat, and leave it at that."

"Fine," he says. "I'll try not to make you nervous anymore if it's such a problem for you. I just didn't realise you were so hung up . . . "

"I am not . . . "

I am already so far behind in this discussion that Pauly doesn't even stay to finish it with me. He is in his sweats and on his way up to the weight room before I even have my shirt off.

"See you upstairs," he says, leaving me alone to dress. I hurry.

By the time I get up there, Pauly is drenched in sweat.

"How did you do that in only five minutes?" I ask.

"Intensity," he says with a knowing wink. "Passion, a high metabolic rate, and a cup of water I poured over my head. I like to get that just-finished-a-marathon look right away."

I look away from sweat boy to size up the facility. The sizing doesn't take too long. There are two treadmills, one Stairmaster, one ergonomic rower, one heavy bag, six ancient Nautilus machines, and a huge mess of free weights spread all over the floor in front of the rack and the full-wall mirror. There is even one of what I believe were called medicine balls a century ago when anybody used them.

"Not exactly state of the art," I say.

"You don't even know what you're looking at," he responds. "It's all in what you *do* with the equipment that makes all the difference. Here, let's play catch."

He, of course, is referring to the medicine ball. "With that? You're joking."

"No way." Pauly picks the ball up, bending at the knees and hoisting like he's powerlifting a ton. Then he brings it up to his chest, walks six paces backward, and launches the thing at me.

It looks, from my angle, like a meteor coming down out of the sky to wipe me out. And, to make it worse, the sight of it in the mirror off to my right pulls my eye just ever so slightly but enough . . .

I am flat. My back is pasted to the floor, and the ball is pasted to my shattered ribs.

"Oh, they are not shattered," Pauly says, laughing from high above me. He is not helping me up. He is not even removing the weight from my chest.

"Yes they are," I insist. "I can't even breathe. When I do – owwwww – my whole left side screams."

"Then just breathe with the other lung for now."

There is no one else in the gym room, thank god, since this was quite embarrassing. But I am not going to beg Paul to unpin me. I maintain my dignity, lie there suffering silently.

He's a sport, though. He kicks the medicine ball off of me, gives me a minute for my lungs to re-inflate, then gives me a hand up.

Pauly goes over and starts pounding on the heavy bag

while I hobble off to the treadmill. I run ten steps before grabbing my side and stopping.

"I can't go any more, Paul," I say.

He stops. "Jesus, are you out of shape. You better become a member."

"Why, so I can come here all the time and have boulders thrown at me?"

"There's a lot more to the place than this."

"It stinks in here too."

"Of course it stinks. It's a men's gym, it's supposed to stink."

"It's not a stink I've ever smelled before."

"Maybe you're just not man enough yet."

"Maybe not. I'm getting out of here, Pauly." I head for the door, and Pauly catches up with me.

"Wait," he says. "Let's just do something else. Let's go down to the pool for some laps."

"They have a pool?"

"Ya. Wanna go?"

"No."

"They also have steam and sauna, and a whirlpool. Hey, that's it, sit in the whirlpool, soak your bruised ribs."

"Broken."

"Fine, soak your broken ribs."

This I like. I follow Pauly through a maze of corridors, past the glass wall of the pool area, past the steam room, the sauna room, the café, the bar.

"For a place with such a crappy gym," I say, "they have some pretty decent extras here."

"Gotta have your priorities," Pauly says.

We are sitting in the jacuzzi for ten minutes before I start to feel a little better. Then I start to feel a lot better. It is the hottest hot tub I have ever been in and I can hardly stand to stay in it but it is irresistible at the same time. The room is kept cooler than the rest of the building, making the hot tub feel all that much stronger, the steam rising off the water's surface and rolling back over my exposed face. I cannot feel my ribs at all anymore. I cannot feel anything at all from the neck down, and I love it. I am a floating head, looking across at Pauly's floating head, with his eyes closed.

Until a person, naked, with a checkered towel over his shoulder, passes through the room without a word, in one door, out the other.

"Pauly," I say as he seems to have slept through it. "Pauly, a naked guy just walked through."

"Ya?" sleepy-eyed Paul says. "Was it the guy with the hog? You should have woke me."

"No, it wasn't him. I think it was that guy Leon."

"Oh," Paul says, and tries to go back to sleep.

"Pauly," I snap and get right to my feet. The blood zooms to my head. Everything goes black, and I sit back down before I fall. "Paul, why would that guy be here?"

Paul shrugs while keeping his eyes closed. "Guess he's a member," he says calmly.

"And where is your brother Henry, anyway?"

"C'mon, Oakley, I got no brother Henry, you know that."

I stand again, more slowly this time. "I want to go," I say. "I've had enough."

"What, we just got here practically. Take a steam."

"I don't wanna take a steam."

"They have an awesome steam here. They're famous for their steam. Take a steam."

"I don't want a steam, I told you."

Paul is once again amused. Because I am nervous.

"You're right," he says. "We should take a sauna instead. I always preferred a sauna myself – better for the skin, I think – and they are equally famous here for their sauna."

"I don't want to take a sauna, dammit, I want to go."

"But I ain't completely boiled yet," he says, raising one leg out of the water for me to see. He looks like a cooked shrimp, the leg all pink and veiny.

I am by now on my way anyway. I have my towel around

my shoulders, my bathing suit dripping a trail behind me as I make for the hallway. Already I am chilled to the bone.

"Fine," Paul calls. "Just give me a couple more minutes, and I'll catch up."

The locker room has, on one wall, a row of shower heads lined up together like the ones in the school gym. There is one guy showering there when I come in, his back to me. There are also, for the more modest among us, a group of separate stalls near the toilets, secluded in the farthest corner from the exit. I grab my soap and shampoo from my locker and head for a private.

They form their own little corridor, the individual showers, with four on the right and four on the left. There is a hook mounted on the tile wall outside each position. The second hook on my right and the third on the left each has a towel hanging from the hook – one a checked towel like the one I had, the other solid blue like Pauly's. I can hear the water spraying hard. Good water pressure. I'm happy.

I walk the short walkway between showers. There are shower curtains hanging from brass rings over each position, but all eight are left open. I pass the blue towel and vaguely notice a figure in there but make sure not to look. I reach the third pair of stalls.

There are two men in the third shower.

I don't have to be bothered by this. It does not have to affect me. This has nothing to do with me. I need not be afraid. They are soaping each other. One man goes up, all the way up, squirting the liquid soap on the other, then down, all the way down, with the soap. The man being washed reaches up and grabs onto the shower nozzle high on the wall behind him. As the other man works on him, he is staring at *me*.

"Shit." I actually say it when I realise I have been frozen there staring at them.

I rush away, head for the last stall, as far away from those two as possible, on the same side of the street as the normal blue towel guy. I throw on the water, make it as hot as possible. I hang my towel, break out the soap and wash myself, scrub and boil and scale myself, as quickly and as thoroughly as I can. I am shaking. I can see this, but cannot feel it because I am again as numb as I was in the hot tub.

Pauly is by now in the stall opposite me. Laughing, naturally. "What are you so worked up about?" he asks in a big whisper.

He knows very well what I'm worked up about. "Listen to that," I whisper back. There are sounds, serious sounds, coming from door number three. "Couldn't they even pull the curtain, for god's sake?"

Pauly laughs. "That wouldn't help. Look." He pulls his own shower curtain closed, pressing it to his naked body.

Not only is the curtain material transparent, it actually works like a magnifying glass, distorting and enlarging.

Paul pops his head around the curtain, looks down at himself. "I gotta get some shorts made out of this stuff."

I am scrubbing so fast the steam coming off my body may actually be smoke. I grab the shampoo, lather up madly.

I don't have my eyes closed for more than ten seconds.

"Hi," he says, and he's right behind me. He is so close I can feel the thin buffer of air between us, like the wrong ends of two magnets, but he does not touch. I can't breathe, much less answer. The shampoo seeps down onto my face because I have stopped scrubbing.

"I'm Henry," he says.

He reaches around from behind.

I'm hard as a diamond. I don't want to be. I have no business being.

"I can explain that," I say, my voice quavering as I grab Henry's wrist and push it away.

"Not necessary, relax," he assures me. His manners are good, except for the way he keeps doing things without asking.

He places his hands on my shoulders and turns me toward him. I move in his grip. I do as directed.

"No," I say, and am very happy to hear myself say it. Because I don't feel in charge.

I don't feel, here, now, like this body I'm in is mine.

I look across to the other stall, to my friend to help me, and he's watching. He's watching, hard, he's watching.

Before I look back down, Henry's mouth is on me.

I open my own mouth to holler at him, but I don't holler at him.

I hesitate.

For three seconds, I don't do a thing.

"I said no," I say firmly, grabbing Henry by the hair and removing him from me.

Henry rises to his feet. He is bigger than me, and older than me, but I have a grip on him like a Rottweiler's bite, and I am ready to do more. I'm not a tough guy by anybody's measure, but I can do this, here and now.

"I don't see what you're so pissed off about," Henry says. "You're the one who hung the checkered towel. And look, Pert shampoo even. You're flying all the flags."

"I like to have a little bounce in my hair, is that all right with you?" I snort, and suddenly see myself there, primed for combat, naked, with a gay man, in the shower. This is such a classic Pauly setup. I look over.

Why isn't he laughing?

Henry pulls his head away, and backs out of the shower. "Listen," he says, "you think I don't know? You think I don't understand? Don't worry, I'm not mad."

"And I'm not worried."

"I'll be in the bar upstairs, if you want to stop in for a glass of suds. On me."

Henry's a gamer, I'll say that.

I tell him I'll think about it. But I have no intention of thinking about it.

We're in the truck on the way back to Whitechurch. We ride all the way without talking about it. Pauly stays on the highway as we pass town, we keep going. We start talking finally.

"Shitty joke, Pauly," I say.

"No joke," he says.

"What was it then?"

"A favour. At least I thought."

"A favour? Pauly, if I wanted guys . . . "

"No, you wouldn't. You never would."

"Well, I don't anyway."

"No offence, Oakley, but really, would you even know?"

"I know, OK."

He laughs at me. Sometimes when Pauly laughs at me it makes me feel better because it reminds me that nothing is that big a deal. Pauly says that all the time, and he's right. But I forget a lot and one kind of laugh he does reminds me.

This is the other kind.

I want to hurt him now.

"I fucked Lilly, is how I know."

Lilly is my best friend. She's Pauly's girlfriend.

I wait for the reaction. I watch his face. I watch him run through the possibilities.

"Lie," he says.

"No lie," I say, and he knows it is true. He also knows that he has never done with Lilly what I have done with Lilly. He probably does not know that she told me. I will tell him that too, some other time when I don't feel like hurting him.

"You slept with my Lilly," he says slowly, nodding, driving. "Next time can you let me know, so I can watch?"

And like that, in his Pauly way, he has ended it. Not the *stuff* that we've churned up, but the tension between him and me. Somehow it feels like we always wind up on the same side of whatever issue, even if the issue is us.

"My dad always told me," I say after one more long pause, "to come tell him right away after I got my first hummer. To tell him how it was. *Now* what am I gonna tell him?"

Pauly grins widely, leans just slightly toward me. "Right, Oak, so . . . what *are* you gonna tell him?"

In lieu of an answer I reach out and clap him on the shoulder. He pulls away violently.

"Hey, keep your hands off me, ya deviate."

He appears to mean it.

BLIND CHANCE

Sam McBratney

Jonathan Fane met the woman in the middle of the night as she wrestled with the serpent called Death. Her name was Miah.

The incident happened in a deserted Birmingham street (for it was half past two in the morning) when, on his way home from work, Fane saw an ambulance parked outside a house. An elderly man leaned out from an upstairs window, sobbing his breath away. Directly below him at street level, the front door of the house lay wide open to reveal a tunnel of light, within which Fane saw a hatstand and a picture of a stag.

Suddenly two people rushed up the long hall with a trolley between them. The young woman at the head of the trolley cursed as she stubbed slightly on the last step into the street. "Why the hell don't they put *ramps* in these places?" Then she caressed the forehead of the old lady who lay on the trolley with a mask over her face.

The lettering in a glass pane above the door said *Sheridan Fold*. Although he passed this place regularly, Fane had not realised until now that it was some sort of sheltered accommodation for old people. The patient on the trolley suddenly tried to sit up, causing a halt to the swift progress to the ambulance.

"There now, you're OK, we'll soon have you right as rain," the woman said, but she was frowning as she fiddled with a loose tube. Her face seemed so intense and full of care that Fane could almost believe he was seeing the face of an angel and his vicarious pride in her brought a lump to his throat. All the while the sobbing continued from above and a blue lamp flicked its intermittent light over the dramatic scene.

Fane felt a thrilling chill run down his spine, the way it used to do when he saw and heard the fire-engine roaring up Prince William Road in Lisburn.

"Can I be of any help?" he asked, coming forward, thinking they might need a lift.

"Yes, just go away," she said with the briefest of glances. "There's always a crowd." Then, to her colleague she added, "Let's get her on board."

The ambulance with its blue light drove away, the hall lights went out, the sobbing stopped, and Fane found himself alone on the deserted pavement.

There hadn't been a crowd, he was thinking. He was the only one and she'd put him firmly in his place, which was fair enough – people under pressure didn't have time to be polite. For some moments he recalled the woman's energy and commitment, and remembered how two or three years ago, when he had done first-aid in the Scouts, he used to run little silent movies in this head in which he rescued someone from drowning or applied the tourniquet that saved a precious life. Why did people say "right as rain"? he wondered.

In the gutter he found a curled up thing which turned out to be a stethoscope. Fane didn't know what to do with it, so he stuffed the various tubes into his pocket and brought it home.

The place that Fane called "home" was a flat with two rooms and a tiny loo. Returning to this place in the dead of night often made him think about the real home he'd left not so long ago. Home, *real* home, was virtually a physical presence with him. He could remember mundane smells and sights and sounds that now almost had the power to make him weep.

There had been tears in his father's eyes when Fane got on the ferry at Larne. He was leaving home at seventeen, not on account of any great crisis, but because it felt like a natural thing to do now that he had finally quit school and had to make his way in the world. His parents explained to their friends that a relative had found him a job – he was going across the water "to work in catering".

"See you, Pop, I'll be in touch," Fane had said, shaking hands, hoisting up his backpack, and his father nodded miserably. Fane knew that the old man did not blame him for leaving school early or for being unemployed. His father was not so much a blamer of people as a blamer of systems and a blamer of Fate. It was even possible, Fane reflected, that he was crying now because he blamed himself, as if he had failed to pass on to his son the genes that would make him a scientific genius or a snooker star.

His mother gave him a hug and a kiss. Fane loved his father more than his mother, although this was something he hoped his mother did not know.

From Birmingham he wrote to them about the job, wrote rather than phoned. He was a kind of assistant in a small hotel, doing all kinds of jobs in and around the lobby – the porter, the receptionist, the cleaner of floors and windows and ashtrays, although he did not mention ugly chores like cleaning up sick in the lift. Oh yes, he had added in a postscript to the last letter, I'm taking a course in hotel management. He knew of the mysterious belief they had in "qualifications". Neither did he mention that the job often involved working nights or that he still had his dream of raising the money to put himself through Drama College.

Now, before settling down with a glass of milk and a raspberry jam sandwich, he cleared a space on the table so that he could put the stethoscope in a safe place. He had no idea whether it was fragile or virtually unbreakable, but there resided in the thing a kind of aura, as if it were a hallowed relic or an icon, and he felt obliged to treat it with care. Had that old woman died? he wondered.

Then he flicked through the channels, searching for

something to watch for an hour or so. This was his routine on the nights when he worked late. As a rule, he rose around noon.

The following day when Fane called at Sheridan Fold a plump lady in a uniform told him that the name of the woman he was looking for was Miah Wessam. "You'd best not leave that gadget here, love. Try for her down at the Health Centre."

Fane thanked her, and asked, "Did the person who was sick last night get better?"

A shake of the head. The plump lady mouthed "Heart, love" meaningfully.

"I'm sorry," said Fane.

A receptionist at the Health Centre paged Miah Wessam, even though he didn't ask her to and he didn't particularly want her to. All of a sudden there she was, walking towards him.

"I'm sorry to disturb you," Fane said, producing the stethoscope from its plastic bag. "I think you dropped this outside Sheridan Fold last night. I was coming home from work when I saw you, that's how I happened to be there. Sometimes I work nights."

"Join the club," said Miah Wessam, taking the stethoscope to examine it.

"It's one of those things I haven't a clue about," Fane went on. "I mean, I don't know if it's worth twenty pounds or five hundred."

"Much closer to the twenty. Yes, I remember you now. One of the paramedics said I was rude to you."

Fane shrugged. "People get in the way, you had work to do."

"Well, this is indeed mine and it's very good of you to bring it back. You're Irish, I think."

"Yes. Well, British too. I'm from the North."

"Oh, the Ulster thing. You're a loyalist."

"Just a citizen of the UK. You wouldn't call somebody from Devon or Yorkshire a loyalist." Fane paused, not wanting to get into all that stuff. "I'm sorry about the old lady who died."

"Yes, of course."

"You did what you could, though. It must be something special to have the kind of knowledge that saves lives. You were like that Greek who wrestled with the serpent, only he couldn't win because the serpent was Death."

"Well that's one way of looking at it," she replied with a smile. "I lose my stethoscope and my patient and you compare me to a Greek hero. Anyway, I thought it was Thor who wrestled with death. Isn't he a Scandinavian?"

"I haven't a baldy clue," admitted Fane.

She was black. Well, not very black; this was an area of uncertainty for Fane. Maybe Asian? Or Egyptian? He reflected that his ignorance would probably be offensive to her, but he had never known a coloured person. Fane grinned, thinking that his Pop being an Orangeman might confuse *her*.

"I guess I should go," he said. "It was nice talking to you. Good Luck!

"And you." She waggled her fingers at him, then walked away down a green corridor. He found himself lingering to watch her slow walk, for lately the motion of graceful women disturbed him pleasurably. The high polished cheekbones, the dark eyes, the amazing smoothness of her forehead after the frown of last night – these were things he had noted and admired also; but of course, he would never see her again.

And yet he did see her again. He saw her three weeks later, at the same early morning hour, in the same street and once more on a Thursday. This time the doors of the ambulance outside Sheridan Fold were already closed when Fane arrived. Some remnant of school learning reminded him that Thursday was Thor's day. These coincidences unsettled him slightly.

The ambulance left without her. From across the street he saw Miah Wessam framed in the yellow light of the hall, talking to two other silhouettes, trying to calm then down. When these others went inside, Fane crossed the road and spoke to her.

"Hello there. It's me again."

There was no surprise in her face; she only nodded, leaned against the wall and said flatly, "Life can be such a bitch." He wondered what had happened.

"You look out on your feet," he said.

"Damn, I should have asked them to get me a taxi. Some of the old people are very upset, I had to stay with them."

"I thought doctors had cars."

"Yes, well, mine's in the garage, sick. A friend rushed me round here."

"*I'll* get you a taxi," said Fane. "Come on, I live round the corner, maybe I could fix you a coffee. Will you do that? Let me make you a coffee?"

"Lead on, Macduff," she said.

On the way Miah Wessam told him that there had been another death at Sheridan Fold, this time an old man of eighty-two. His wife had died three weeks ago to the day, almost to the hour. She had been the same age, eighty-two years old.

"That was the night I first saw you," Fane remarked. "Amazing coincidence."

She said, "Hmm."

In the flat she was very quiet while Fane phoned for a taxi and made some tea. He was glad that she preferred tea because he was not convinced that other people enjoyed his version of coffee. Each sat at one end of the rickety table he'd bought at a second-hand shop, a plate of biscuits between them. By good luck he was able to produce a carton of fresh milk.

"Tea OK?"

"Hmm. Tea's tea."

"Was he . . . alive when you got there?" asked Fane.

"Oh yes. He talked to me." She gave a laugh he could not explain, then slipped two fingers through the handle of a Dulux-dog mug. She was all of a piece, motionless. If she gave a start her whole body would jolt, the tea would spill. The more he watched her, the more certain he felt that she was not behaving normally. But he loved the stillness in her face and the fullness of her lips.

"Do you want a ginger biscuit?"

"No."

"I'm a sucker for dunking ginger biscuits, but they melt if you don't time it right. Then you get this horrible mush at the bottom of the cup."

"What am I doing here? This is completely bizarre."

"Maybe because it's the night-time," agreed Fane. "I've noticed that things are different when everybody else is asleep. Sometimes I think it's a bit like being in the theatre. The first time you saw me you said, 'There's always a crowd.' You can only get a crowd of one at night-time. This doesn't make any sense to you, I suppose, but I just think that people are different by night."

She seemed to be listening but her mind was elsewhere. Twice she had wrestled with death and she had lost and now on an impulse he took one of her hands in his, rocked it gently, then let it go. What gave him the right, or indeed the courage, to behave in this way, he had no idea. "Are you going back to someone who will take care of you?"

"Three of us share a house. I think I heard the taxi. Will you be an angel and lend me ten pounds? I really did think I'd be going back with the ambulance."

Fane leaned out of the window to wave at the taxi-driver in case he wakened the neighbourhood, then gave her two five pound notes, saying lightly, "There you are, just call me Gabriel. The question is, what interest do I get on my loan?"

"Is Gabriel your name?"

"No, you said 'be an angel'. Gabriel's the big cheese among angels."

"Oh I see. And who is the angel of death?"

"Never met the guy. I'm no expert on angels."

Now she gave a relaxed giggle, perhaps brought on by

the absurdity of discussing angels at three o'clock in the morning. Before Miah Wessam left she gave him a piece of paper bearing her name, an address and the message: *IOU ten pounds plus interest, call tomorrow at two.*

When she had gone, something else of her remained in this flat: the smell of an angel who had wrestled with death and eaten curry.

The house where Miah Wessam lived was situated in a leafy cul-de-sac beside a public park. A nice little niche, thought Fane. Some of the trees soaring out of the pavement were almost as high as the houses. The bell in the front door was one of those annoying things that didn't seem to ring when he pressed it, but she opened the door almost immediately.

"Ah! Entrez," she said in mock French.

"Merci bucket," replied Fane, likewise.

He followed her into a room where a huge couch strewn with cushions faced an electric fire set in a fake fireplace. Two wine bottles on the table had ugly collars of wax from the well-burned candles rammed into their necks. A bay window let in generous amounts of afternoon light, and in this light her hair was so black that it seemed radiant. How could that be? he wondered.

"You're staring at me as if I've shrunk," she said.

"Sorry. I've always been a bit of a starer."

"Anyway, I haven't thanked you properly for being so kind. So what's your name?"

"Fane. Jonathan Fane."

"Well, Jonathan Fane, I've got your money. *And* your interest, you'll be glad to hear."

As she reached for a little dish on the mantelpiece, Miah Wessam's clothes became taut around her body and Fane longed to be close to her. Sooner or later there would come a time, a first time for him to make love to someone, and Fane had always suspected that he would have to be shown how, have to be guided through the process like a nervous and clumsy novice. Now he learned that this was not necessarily so, for the physical presence of a woman like Miah Wessam would empower him fully – had done so already even as he stood watching her.

She turned and knew of his arousal. No stethoscope would she need to know the quickness in his heart.

"Can I say something?" Fane said, blushing. "To me you're beautiful. That's why I was staring."

A little grin; and then she said, "You make it sound as though the rest of the world thinks I'm ugly."

"No, they couldn't think that," Fane rushed to say, the words tripping out, "I've been thinking about the way we met. You know – that man dying at the same time as his wife. All those coincidences."

"It wasn't a coincidence."

"That's what I mean!" agreed Fane. "Too many things happened together. After eighty-two years his heart and her heart stopped beating at the same time, on the same day and within three weeks. But if it wasn't coincidence, then what was it?"

"What do *you* think it was?" she asked him quietly.

"I don't know. My pop says people are only straws in the wind; he believes in fate. Things are meant to be." Fane laughed, embarrassed. "Maybe we were destined to meet, who knows?"

Miah Wessam came towards him and put the money into his breast pocket. "I'm glad we did meet; you helped me at a difficult time."

She was within reach of his arms now. "It was a Thursday both times, remember?" he pointed out. "And you were right, it was Thor who wrestled with Death. Think of all the things that had to happen! I mean, you have to admit it's strange. If you hadn't lost your stethoscope, if your car hadn't broken down . . . " He paused. "Do you think I'll see you again?"

As if to admire the symmetry in the patterns of the rug beneath her feet, Miah Wessam dipped her head for some moments; then she spoke again with quiet deliberation.

"When I got there – to Sheridan Fold, I mean – Mr Conrad was very frightened. What happened wasn't coincidence at all!" Her eyes flicked upwards, a single glance. "Or destiny either.

It wasn't a coincidence because he chose the moment. To him, that was the most natural time in the world for his life to finish."

"I don't see what you mean."

"He was married at twenty-one. They had been together for sixty-one years and he didn't want to live any more so he took tablets. It's as simple as that."

"But he was alive when you got there."

"Yes, he was."

"You said you talked to him."

"He wouldn't let me do anything; he begged me just to watch and be there. He talked to his Annie as if she was in the next room, waiting for him to come through and join him. Actually, I couldn't bear it. He wouldn't even tell me what he'd taken and I told myself it was too late anyway . . . Maybe you're right when you said that things are different in the night."

Once more Fane stared at her. "You mean, you didn't do anything?"

"I held his hand."

At that moment Fane had no idea what to say. Vaguely he was aware that somehow she had demolished the very idea of what he had imagined her to be. Nor did she help him. She only stared back. When the silence threatened to become ridiculous, he turned towards the door.

"Wait. Don't go without your interest!" So saying, she pressed upon him a packet of gingernut biscuits. It was a small kindness, a continuation of his own little joke and Fane acknowledged it with a half-smile; but once more he felt dismissed, a crowd of one.

Outside, kids were coming home from school. The autumn sun cast sharp-edged shadows in his path and he knew that she had allowed the old man to switch out his own light. *And who is the angel of death?* she had asked him.

Fane shoved the ginger biscuits deep into a pocket. An anger of sorts gripped him, but whether it was against her or himself or the blind chance that had brought them briefly together, he didn't truly know.

A TIGHT TEAM

Gretta Mulrooney

I suppose I'd always thought that if life changed suddenly it would be because of illness or an accident; being knocked down by a car or finding I had leukaemia. I'd imagined the death bed scene with myself propped on snowy pillows, pale but brave, or propelling my wheelchair valiantly along the street while passers-by exchanged glances of admiration.

There's an old question that crops up now and again; if you had to lose one of your senses, which would you choose not to part with? I've always said my sight; I like to see what's coming towards me. My father, who loves music, would say his hearing and my closest friend May, who loves to eat, would say taste. But of course it's a pointless question because in real life you don't get to choose your misfortune.

During that Saturday evening, after Estelle had arrived and my world had tilted to an odd angle, I thought of May's brother Jack who was run over by a motor bike that had come up behind him; he had his Walkman on and didn't hear or see anything. One minute he was cycling along picturing the chicken supper he was going to buy, the next he was lying in the road minus two fingers and with facial wounds that would scar.

On that Saturday, up to the point when Estelle surfaced, my family was going about its usual routine. I was absorbed in my weekend job, helping my father, who's a vet, in his surgery. My mother does the book-keeping for the business, orders supplies, answers the phone, runs the appointments diary. We were a tight team, my father had always said; it was good to keep things in the family. He'd converted an old saying about prayer to, "the family that works together stays together". It was taped over the computer in the office.

I busied around, calming cats, checking notes were ready, wiping down surfaces and sterilising instruments, unaware that trouble was speeding up behind me. If my father seemed a little distracted I put it down to the fact that the surgery was busy and he was having to concentrate. My mother was flushed – but then she often is because she's menopausal and regularly has to cool off with a battery-operated pocket fan. We had a rushed lunch – sandwiches in our hands – and watched five minutes of the News before returning to work.

You see, we were just a family getting on with life; slightly unusual for Ireland because I was an only child, but then that was accounted for by my mother's unreliable fallopian tubes. If I'd been interviewed for a national survey on family life I would have said that my parents had always been frank with me; in fact I probably knew details of my mother's gynaecological problems that I'd rather have been ignorant of and when my father had been debating whether or not to go into partnership I'd been fully involved in the discussions. We rarely quarrelled, I was paid well for my Saturdays and was allowed to do what I liked socially as long as I was home by midnight. Compared to some of my friends I had problem-free parents; I would listen to accounts of open hostilities about pocket money, battles over bedrooms, fights to do with clothes and I have to confess that sometimes I invented arguments at home in order to make domestic life sound more interesting. I often go out with May on Saturday nights but my father had asked if I'd stay in and have a meal with them on that particular evening because a student was coming round. He frequently takes a veterinary student on at the practice for a couple of months and we always give them the once-over by inviting them for dinner. That was OK with me; it had been pouring all day and May had a heavy cold. We'd probably only have been sprawling in her room surrounded by tissues, nasal sprays and the reek of menthol.

After we'd closed the surgery I indulged in a deep hot bath while rain whipped at the windows. Submerged in foam, I completed a cover-to-cover reading of the magazines May had swapped with me. My radio was on but I could hear the faint chink of dishes as my mother bustled in the kitchen and my father's deep growl accompanying a baritone in *La Traviata*. They were familiar sounds that had been in the background for as long as I could remember. I felt contented, secure in the snug knowledge that all was as it should be. I'm not sure now that I'll ever feel like that again; the girl relaxing in the bath seems like someone from another life, another time.

As I dressed I heard the doorbell and my father walking down the hall. I brushed my hair, taking a last look in the mirror. It seems to me that I should have noticed a shadow at my shoulder but there was just my reflection, rosy faced from the bathroom steam, freckled, with clear eyes lacking the knowledge that was about to cloud them.

Downstairs, a tall, slim young woman was standing by the fire, a sherry glass in her hand. She was dressed all in grey; trousers, shirt and long jacket, and her waist length blue-black hair flowed straight from a centre parting. My father turned from pouring himself a whisky and said, "Jo, this is Estelle, Estelle Blanc. The person I told you about," he added as she glanced at him.

Blanc was entirely the wrong surname because her skin was the colour of hazelnuts and her large luminous eyes a shade of treacle toffee. We said hallo and shook hands. She had an English accent and a husky voice, as if she smoked too much.

My father is more at ease with animals than with people and was always nervous if we had to entertain. He twirled his glass around, slopping whisky, and said something about the dreadful weather. Estelle told us that it had been sunny in London when she left and I was surprised that he hadn't mentioned that she was an English student as we'd only ever had home-grown ones before. My mother hurried in, red in the face, and announced that dinner was ready.

"Do you want a window open?" my father asked her when we'd sat at the table.

She shook her head, slicing away at a chicken and mushroom pie. Drops of perspiration were standing out on her forehead. I'd never seen her this bad and thought that maybe there was a crisis point in the menopause. "Are you not feeling well?" Estelle asked her. She wore three heavy silver bangles on her right wrist which seemed too ornate against her plain suit.

I held my breath because, given an opening, my mother was likely to launch into a full description of her most florid symptoms, but she concentrated on serving up the pie and said diffidently that it was just her time of life.

I can't pinpoint when it dawned on me that there was something odd about this Saturday dinner. As we made our way through the first course the conversation was stilted. Estelle commented on the plates and my mother coughed, patting her chest and saying that they'd been handed down from her grandmother. My father recounted a comic story, which I'd heard him tell before, about a talking parrot, only on this occasion he fluffed several of the funniest lines so that the humour was lost. The scraping of cutlery filled awkward silences. Estelle was wearing a spicy perfume that drifted across the table every time she lifted a hand to flick her hair back. I could taste it on my lips as I ate. I looked at my father; the usual script was that after some initial pleasantries he would get the prospective students to tell us about themselves, their background and experience to date. He was examining his food, turning over a piece of mushroom as if it was a rare species he'd never come across before. My mother had taken her fan out and the whirring sounded like a trapped cranefly's wings beating against glass. Estelle looked at me quizzically and I filled the gap, telling her that I was at school. "What made you want to be a vet?" I asked her, picturing her in the surgery with her hair coiled up. It would be a tremendous weight on the top of her head. Her burnished skin would set off the clinical whiteness of her coat.

She put her knife and fork down. "Pardon?" she said sharply.

"Why did you decide . . . ?" I started to repeat myself but my father's voice came in from the background, saying, "Oh, oh now . . . "

There was a silence. I looked round the table. Estelle was staring at my father. He was worrying the handle of his knife. A small red blotch had bloomed on his neck. My mother's eyes glistened behind a watery film. I caught a sudden sniff of fear; I knew it well from the terrified animals who struggled before the anaesthetic soothed their troubles.

"She doesn't know, does she?" Estelle said to my father. "You haven't told her." She gripped the table edge, her bracelets clashing.

He shook his head and pushing his chair back, stood up. He steadied himself with one hand on the table, then moved to the window and looked out. My mother took in a deep, ragged-sounding breath.

"Shall I . . . ?" she said to my father.

He put his hand up, still turned from us. "No, no, I'll . . . give me a minute."

"You're sixteen, aren't you?" Estelle asked me.

"Yes."

"Well, he's only had years to tell you. I suppose we can

give him another minute." She reached for her bag. "Mind if I smoke?" she asked my mother.

"Tell me what? What's going on?" I turned to Estelle. She was lighting up a thin, dark brown cigarette. "Aren't you a veterinary student?" She shook her head at me. "I wouldn't know one end of an animal from another. I'm in the retail business."

My mother touched my sleeve. "Estelle has come for another reason."

"What?"

She made a little movement with her hands and then cupped them around her beetroot cheeks. My father moved back to the table, paddling his hands in his pockets as if he was searching for something. He sat down again and spoke to me but he wasn't looking in my eyes; he fixed his gaze on a point over my left shoulder.

"Um, many years ago, must be – let me see – twenty one years now, I had a relationship with someone called Monique. She . . . we . . . had a daughter and she was named Estelle."

He took a long drink of water. The fire hissed and a spark flashed briefly. I had that sensation that comes when flu is waiting to pounce; shivery, then warm, with everything slightly out of focus. My mother re-filled my glass with water and nudged it towards me. I watched the bubbles on the surface, aware of Estelle's long fingers lying beside her lighter. She had the kind of nails I'd always craved: symmetrical and strong with pale, even cuticles.

The last bubble popped. "So Estelle is my half-sister?" I said and my voice sounded far away.

My father nodded.

"Hi," Estelle said. "Hi, Jo."

I didn't reply. There was a sourness in my throat and I thought that if I didn't sit very still I might be sick. That was when I had the memory of Jack and the motorbike and his fingers lying in the road. They were watching me, except for my father. When Estelle had spoken my name he had covered his ears. I sipped at my glass.

"Did you know?" I asked my mother.

"I did, yes. Not when it . . . it happened. Your father was away on a course then. He told me when Estelle was born."

I managed a quick mental calculation. "And you were married then?"

"Yes."

I felt hot and clammy. Tiny spots were dancing across my eyes. I drank more water and held the glass against my forehead for a minute. I had been born ten years after my parents married. During those ten years my mother had had all kinds of tests and operations so that she could get pregnant. While she'd been going through all that my father had had a child with someone else.

"We thought it was time you knew," my father said, a pleading note in his voice.

I couldn't look at him. I knew he wanted me to.

"I thought it was *high* time you knew," Estelle added, "He said he'd tell you before I arrived. Sorry about the shock."

A kind of coolness came over me then. Maybe it was the way she said "he" quite casually, with familiar ownership. I felt icy towards her and them.

"I'd like to be on my own with my parents," I said.

She made a kind of tutting noise through her teeth but she got up and my father showed her into the sitting room. When he came back he poked at the fire before perching on his chair.

"Where has she been all these years?" I asked him.

"In London, with her mother. Now she's coming to work in Dublin for a while. Jo, I'm sorry you've found out like this. I've wanted to tell you but somehow . . . the time never seemed right."

I didn't want to hear how sorry he was. "Did you see her while she was growing up?"

"Once a year, when I was at the conference in London."

He attended an annual vets' meeting every February. My mother had never gone with him, although some people's partners did. She'd always said she disliked flying. She was drawing lines on the tablecloth with her finger.

"Didn't you mind?" I asked her.

"Mind!" she said, with a little laugh. "Of course I minded. But you can't ignore a child." She blinked and shook her head impatiently. "I was just dreading telling you. I wanted you to know a long time ago but your father . . . "

We'd sat around that table so many times, discussing things, arguing amicably. Usually our chairs were drawn in and I'd be lying with my elbows stretched out. Sometimes, when I got the better of him, my father would flick a piece of food at me and I'd catapult it back; then my mother would intervene, laughing, saying we were savages. Now our chairs were angled away and we were avoiding each other's glances.

"I can't believe you kept this from me," I said. "All those years of saying we're a tight unit, sharing everything. What is it you've always asked at breakfast, Dad? 'What's today's agenda?' All the time you had your own secret little agenda." Their names kept repeating in my ears; *Monique* and *Estelle*. Different, exotic on the tongue.

What other house had my father been visiting all these years? Had he sung the same songs to Estelle as he'd sung to me, played the same games with her? She would have sat on his knee chuckling as he made finger shadows on the wall; a rabbit's waggling ears, a beaky bird of prey. I looked at him but I couldn't see him. The man opposite was a miserable-looking stranger.

He rubbed his forehead. "How can I explain? It got harder as years went by. Sometimes, in between visits, it all seemed unreal, as if Estelle didn't exist. I didn't want to make you unhappy."

I wanted him to explain but I couldn't bear to listen. "You didn't even tell me before she came! What were you going to do, write me a note and hand it to me with pudding?" They both sat silent with numb expressions. I didn't want my parents looking like this: sad, uncertain, guilty. I'd never seen them that way. It frightened me. Panic overtook me and I knew I had to get away. I ran for a coat and dashed out, banging the door.

It was still raining steadily. I didn't mind because I was crying by then, huge fat tears that were camouflaged by raindrops. I walked and walked, right into the city and down by the quays. My feet were saturated, my hair plastered to my head but I just kept moving through that liquid world. It felt as if someone had punched me and I had to take little breaths. I'd always believed what my parents told me; they had seemed as solid and dependable as rock. Now I wondered if there were other things that had been kept from me; did my mother know more secrets concerning my father? After all, it was she who had once warned me about the hazards of lying; tell one, she'd said, and it can grow and then it's easier to tell the next. I hadn't realised she was speaking from experience. Finally, exhausted, I stopped at a little café for a cup of tea but I couldn't taste it. I watched myself drink, thinking: oh, look at that girl, you can see she's had a terrible shock. The thought that other people might notice and pity me drove me back into the night. I plodded home because it was late and I had nowhere else to go, but as I drew near the house I saw that it had changed; the curtained windows looked masked and the tall sycamore draped a shadowy veil over the porch. I almost expected my key not to fit the lock.

Four Saturdays have gone by. I'm just like Jack was after his accident; I find myself moving around cautiously, wary

107

of sudden noises. My skin feels too thin, as if it would bruise easily. I go to bed early and sleep late, wrapping myself in a sheet cocoon. I'm glad that winter is here because I can bury myself in layers of clothing, bandaging myself for protection.

I've got a new Saturday job, working in a shoe shop. Now I smell of sweatened leather instead of antiseptic at the end of the day. My father didn't say anything when I told him he'd have to find someone else. My parents give me lowered, careful looks. If I ask for information they offer it. I'm like someone taking a medication, gradually building up the dosage. I hate the taste of the medicine but I find I need it; so I know that Monique is Mauritian, that my father gave her money over the years for Estelle's upbringing, that Estelle is in the city for a while managing the launch of a new English clothes store. She'd like to get to know me, they've said, but I don't respond to the tiny lift of hope in their voices. I think that she visits sometimes when I'm at school; I'm sure that I've caught a trace of her perfume downstairs.

May is the only person I've told about it and I've sworn her to secrecy. She says that maybe if I get to know Estelle I'll like her, that in time it might be good to have a sister. She showed me a letter to an agony aunt on exactly the same subject in one of her magazines. I listen to her but she might as well be speaking a foreign language. She thinks that I'll feel better, knowing that this has happened to other people, but I don't. It's my home that that perfume is lingering in.

Perhaps I will get to know Estelle but May and my parents are missing the point. It's my father who is the stranger to me and that is why my skin is so thin. Whatever happens, it will be a while before I'll be ready to remove the bandages and, like Jack, I'll have a scar.

SUMMER LOVE

Joan O'Neill

It was only when I returned to school after a week's absence last year that I realised how everything had changed. Suddenly I was the most popular girl in Saint Mary's, and my popularity lay in the aura of mystery and danger that surrounded me. Whatever kind of success or achievement I had aspired to academically was thwarted. From now on I would be known and remembered as the girl who ran away, a scandal that would live with me throughout my school years.

I will never forget the first day back. Walking down the long corridor, the noisy classrooms on the left, girls all talking, giggling together. The sudden hush as I approached, the nods from some of my classmates, the whispers as I passed, the "Did you hear?" or "Wouldn't you think?" a long sigh of disapproval trailing in my wake. I had done something that had set me apart for the rest of my school career. Worse still, and what really maddened everyone, was that I refused to talk about it, or give any details about where I'd gone or what I'd done. My sister Emily filled me in on the variations of the rumours she'd heard. But what struck me most about my return, or forced return, was the normality of my home without me, the sense of life going on. As I let myself in the front door there was no sign of the chaos caused by my absence. My little brother Peter's toy bricks were strewn across the hall, and there was the sound of splashing water and the whoops of his excited laughter from the bathroom. Not only was life going on, it was being enjoyed.

With relief I saw that Emily was home. Her schoolbag was lying in the corner, crammed with books, her coat thrown casually on top of it, her muddy Doc Martens carelessly askew under the hall table. All testaments to the busyness of her life.

Passing the mirror I caught sight of my reflection. The dirty face, stringy hair and rumpled clothes made me want to cry. But the deep and profound change that I felt had taken place in me was not obvious in the mirror. Straightening my shoulders, I reminded myself "Don't be nervous", a maxim I had chanted all the way home in the bus until it was now a rhythm in my head. Before I got to the door of the living-room my mother came running down the stairs, her head tilted in the direction of the kitchen.

"Becky," she cried, stumbling on the last step when she saw me.

Rushing forward she grabbed me, squeezed me tight, then stood back to verify it was really me. Gripping me by my shoulders she proceeded to shake the daylights out of me as she started "Where have you been?", her voice so shrill that it brought the rest of the family rushing out, headed by my father.

"We were worried sick. Weren't we, Jim?" She looked at him for verification. "We had the police out searching for you."

My father was standing there, his face composed, distant, unforgiving.

"Where were you?" he asked in his most reasonable, tolerant voice.

I looked at him, tight-lipped, defiant.

"If you won't talk to us, you'll have to talk to someone in authority," he said.

My mother remained silent, her anger obvious in the tightness of her mouth.

I had gone to Liverpool on the boat. I had looked it up on the map. It was close enough to get to but far enough to get away from my parents. According to my calculations I had enough money saved to pay the fare and to stay there for several days. I had to go, it was where Adam Slater, my boyfriend, was.

The first time I saw Adam Slater was on stage in the Community Centre in Swords. He was the lead singer in a band called Asylum and he was lolling back on a chair in blue jeans, a check shirt, earrings, and a gold chain around his neck, playing snatches of tunes, a sort of warming up session before the gig when Tara and I arrived to audition for the backing group. He was the most beautiful fella I'd ever laid eyes on. Johnny Depp came to mind – his eyes were dark, brooding, his cheekbones sharp, and his hair long and curly. But it was the softness of his mouth when he smiled that made me go after him, shamelessly.

My heart was beating so hard when I clambered on to the stage that I was afraid he would hear it in my ribcage. I began strumming my guitar but when I opened my mouth to sing my voice broke. The words of the song came out squeaky. Adam laughed and said "Have you been drinking?" then turned and said something to the drummer. A remark that made them both laugh loudly. But it didn't put me off. I started again. When I finished he nodded in Tara's direction. "Now I'd like to hear you sing."

"What's your name?" he asked at the end of her song.

"Tara Murphy," she replied.

"Yours?" he looked at me.

"Rebecca Delaney," I said, wishing it was Cheryl Crow.

"I'd like to hear you sing together," he said.

Happy to oblige, we sang "Hey Now", a song we had practised together.

"Stay behind afterwards," Adam told us when we were through. "I want a word with you both."

I couldn't believe my ears because I hadn't wanted to go to the audition in the first place. Tara had persuaded me. She was keen on Andy, the drummer, and because she was one of the most popular girls in the school I hadn't the courage to say no.

"It'll be cool," she had said. "You'll be sorry if you miss it."

I soon discovered that Adam wasn't only the lead singer. He was in charge of this newly-formed band as well. Whenever there was a problem he would sort it out. He decided about the lighting, the sound system, the venues, who to hire and fire. I couldn't take my eyes off him.

After our audition we sat on a bench against the wall sipping cokes, trying to look aloof, hiding our insecurity in small-talk and waiting for the gig to begin. Eventually I got up to dance. I felt Adam looking at me when he thought I wasn't noticing.

"How long are you playing the guitar?" he asked me later, backstage.

"Oh, a couple of years," I said casually. "I started on the piano but it was too slow so I thought the guitar might suit me better."

"Well, I might as well be honest. It's not your guitar-playing that captivates me. It's your voice. You have a sureness of note that's uncommon in a girl so young."

"I'm sixteen," I said.

Adam laughed. "Your voices blend well together. Maybe you'd give us a dig-out Friday night? We're playing in Swords and we're badly stuck."

Startled, I opened my mouth to say something but found I was tongue-tied. This gorgeous creature looking at us with those smouldering eyes wanted us to play in his band!

"Brush up on your guitar playing between this and then," he said.

"Yeh, we will," Tara nodded enthusiastically.

In spite of my nervousness I found myself smiling. Tara ran off gushing with the news to Andy. I waited for her outside the Community Hall, subdued by the suddenness of success and fame as I saw it.

"What do you think?" Tara asked as we walked home.

"Brilliant," I said. "I can't wait."

"We'll have to practise every spare minute we can between now and Friday."

I nodded.

"What'll your Mum say?" Tara looked at me anxiously, knowing how conservative my mother was.

"I won't tell her. I'll say I'm practising for the school choir."

It was a shame about the guitar. Not that I didn't appreciate it at the time. A beautiful, expensive Christmas present like that. Dad thought it would encourage me with my singing lessons. Only after I had got it did I realise that I wasn't guitar-playing material. The word "practise" undermined my enthusiasm every time I heard it.

We got through the first gig in a trance. I took my gear and make-up bag to Tara's house. Painstakingly I applied my make-up, outlining my eyes with black eyeliner. It made me look older, more wordly-wise. I combed my long hair, securing it in place with plenty of hair spray, and wore the new red lycra top I'd bought in Topshop, my black micro mini, black stockings and boots to match.

"How do I look?" I asked Tara, gazing into her full-length mirror.

"Deadly. I'd kill for a figure like yours," Tara said, applying a dab of lip gloss, not meaning a word of it.

With her heart-shaped face and flyaway blonde hair she was the best-looking girl in the school, as well as the most popular. Standing there, in her long black skimpy dress, her dark make-up and silver jewellery, she looked drop dead gorgeous.

The gig was in a marquee in Swords. The inside was a bright, dancing balloon, its undulating walls all shimmering colours like splinters of glass. Groups of girls stood around near the entrance, wreathed in smiles, pretending it didn't matter that the boys were keeping their distance. The fellas stayed together at the far side of the tent, clean, dressed up, their wet hair spiked with Brylcream. Asylum were on stage wearing peacock blue shirts and jeans. The lights were too bright, the music too loud. When Adam beckoned to us I froze. Suddenly the waiting, the agonising suspense, the yearning for everything to happen, reached right down to my toes. I felt as if I was outside myself, watching. The dilemma of singing in front of such a huge audience made me jittery.

Tara nudged me. "Come on," she hissed.

We moved together, slowly merging in with the rest of the band, camouflaged by their colourful clothes and musical instruments.

The dancing began, the crowd moved towards the stage. I tilted my head against the glare of the light and watched Adam as he sang, "Don't Look Back in Anger", one of my favourite Oasis songs.

I watched the intense way he held his guitar, as if it were part of him, and the various ways he used it, twisting it, turning it, slapping the side of it, his strong fingers firm on the strings. His eyes were on mine as he teased out the slow, sentimental words of "Champagne Super Nova". We joined in, strumming our guitars, swaying with the music. I was floating, in Seventh Heaven, my eyes only on him. No one else existed.

When the dance ended I went in search of the cloakroom and splashed water on my forehead to cool my scarlet face. Why was I so nervous? I asked myself, smoothing down my hair and refreshing my make-up.

"Hurry up, I'm burstin' ", Tara called outside the door.

"You were great," Adam said as he helped us into the back of the van to take us home.

All the way there we discussed the band, the various instruments, the phrasing, the rhythms, sitting propped against the musical instruments and sound systems.

Next day was Saturday. During lunch hour I ran around Eddie Rocket's where I worked in my free time, serving customers, perspiration trickling down my back, its dampness cold against my skin. When there were only a few tables left I slowed down.

"It's getting quiet," Tracy, the Manageress said. "Might as well take yourself off. I'll finish up here."

"Thanks." I quickly removed my red cap and apron.

The lights were coming on over the town as I left the building. My arms and legs ached and I was sweltering. I set off towards home without thinking, glad the day was over. Suddenly I spotted Adam out of the corner of my eye. He was standing beside a parked motorbike. I looked away, immediately feeling the compulsion to look back again.

"Hi!" he called out to me.

"Hello," I said surprised. "Are you waiting for someone?"

"Yeah. You."

He smiled and shifted from one foot to the other.

"Coming for a spin?" he asked.

"Only if you go fast," I teased, embarrassed in my stupid uniform.

"You're fine," he said. "Here's a helmet, hop on."

The roar of the engine, the tilt and swoosh of the big bike as it rounded the corner sent my heart soaring. We raced down Church Street, me pressed against Adam's back, my arms clenched tight around his waist. Exhilarated by the blast of air, the powerful machine vibrating beneath us, we moved in unison through the quiet, narrow streets. Free, flying, wanting this to go on forever.

"Scared?" he called over his shoulder.

"No," I shouted, my voice dying on the wind.

Out in the countryside the sound rent the quiet as the Harley Davidson swallowed up the miles. Eyes smarting, hair streaming beneath our helmets, we swooped down deserted roads. A rush of pure joy shot through my body as the speedometer tilted towards ninety. I threw my head back to gaze at the emerging stars. The world was ours and ours alone.

We stopped outside an all-night café.

"Hungry?" Adam asked.

The whole place seemed to shudder to a halt when we stepped inside, Adam in his leathers, his hair tousled, his eyes brilliant, me in my black trousers, red and white striped shirt, sleeves rolled up.

He ordered milkshakes, burgers, chips. We ate like savages, washing our meal down with coke. Sitting opposite him I felt important.

"How would you like to play with the band for the summer?" Adam asked casually when we'd finished eating.

I looked at him to see if he was joking but he was serious.

"I could give you some guitar lessons. That is if you're interested . . . "

Interested. This gorgeous fella was offering to give me a job for the summer and guitar lessons to boot.

"But there's my job," I stammered.

My earnings from my part-time job supplied me with school books and pocket money, but it curtailed my mobility at weekends.

"Give it up. We'll pay you," he smiled.

"What about Tara?"

"Andy's going to ask her."

A week later I arrived at Adam's flat with my guitar for rehearsal.

"Let's begin," he said, putting his arms around me to show me how to hold the guitar properly, so that I could get

116

the best sound from the strings. We practised fingering the notes until they became clearer and my fingers hurt.

"I'm hopeless," I said, frustrated.

"Don't put yourself down," Adam said. "Relax, take your time and it'll come to you."

He liked me. I could see it in his eyes. He was about twenty-one years old, five years older than me; it seemed to bring out a protective brotherly tenderness in him. I went home in a dream-like state, unsure of whether my feet actually touched the ground or not, caring about nothing except Adam Slater and his band.

It started slowly. I'd go to his house for lessons and we'd talk afterwards. He was full of opinions that weren't just about music. He knew about paintings too and could explain how different colours and textures worked on canvas. He was my teacher, bestower of all good things.

Outside my gate one night, after the third lesson, he kissed me. In his arms I crumpled, shedding my inhibitions as he held me tight, letting each moment take its course. I didn't tell my parents about Adam or the band. No questions asked. No answers given.

The summer flew by and I was entranced by my new freedom. I lived in an almost magical daze of well-being as a member of the band, learning to vocalise with a variation of songs, building up confidence. Adam and I became an item in the band and at parties and I continued to take instruction devotedly from him – and not only guitar lessons. He introduced me to all sorts of new things – new foods, drinks – we walked and talked on the beach, listened to the silence. The more I sat with him on the dunes or in his flat and plucked the strings of my guitar, exercised my vocal chords, the more he discarded his reticence about my age. His world became mine and I saw few of my schoolfriends except Tara, who was preoccupied with Andy.

Towards the end of the summer something went wrong.

Some little thing too unshaped to give it expression. It was more of a feeling than anything else, but I suspected that Adam's reticence about my age had come to the fore again.

"We'll be moving on soon," he said one evening as we strolled along the beach.

Startled, I turned to him.

He continued walking.

"We're forming a proper band. Taking on new talent, letting some of the fellas go, recording an album. Going upmarket for our British tour."

"British tour. When?"

"Autumn."

"But we'll be back at school."

"I know." Adam looked into the distance. "I did say it was only for the summer months."

"Yeah, I know. But what about you and me?"

Adam stopped walking and turned to me. He put his hands on my shoulders.

"You're lovely, Becky," he said. "Truly lovely, but I don't want us to get too serious. You know what I mean . . . "

I was crushed. I couldn't believe what I was hearing.

"Look, Becky. You're young. Far too young for a serious relationship. You need to spread your wings."

"I don't feel too young for you," I said.

Suddenly I felt lonely, vulnerable, like when my mother left me at Auntie Betty's when she was having Peter. Before I could stop myself, I was crying, the tears running down my face . . . desperately lonely for Adam, though he was right by my side.

Adam held me.

"I'm sorry," he said. "I don't want you to be sad. But don't you see, your age makes it difficult. I can't take you on tour and obviously I can't stay here forever. The band's moving on and I've got to move with it."

"So you said."

Adam paced up and down, his movements graceful, his face frowning as my world caved in around me.

"You should have thought of all this sooner," I shouted at him. "Before we became involved."

When he saw the thunderous expression on my face, he laughed.

"Listen, Becky, you're innocent, sweet. The lessons were part of something romantic and irresistible. I didn't think you'd take it so seriously."

"How was I supposed to take it?" I shouted. "With a grain of salt?"

He kept calm, talking in a reasonable voice. The more he talked the more I felt let down by his know-it-all attitude. I turned to walk away.

He followed me.

"I'll take you home," he said.

"No, I'd rather walk," I said, walking faster. As soon as he was out of sight I ran all the way home, tears streaming down my cheeks.

"The maddening thing is," I said to Tara, who had also been dropped by the band, "their fanciful notion of who to invite to Liverpool and who to leave out. Like a game or something. Only with people's emotions. It's disgusting."

"We couldn't have gone anyway," Tara said, drying her eyes. "We've got to finish school."

Suddenly the summer holidays were over. The band was gone.

"They'll be back," Tara said. "Andy promised. Not that I'll wait around for him. The fellas in some of the other bands are much better looking."

Although Tara tried to sound blasé she didn't fool me. She was as devastated as I was.

The first week back at school was a nightmare. Trying to act normal after such an eventful summer was impossible. On the Monday of the second week I left the house as usual, ostensibly to go to school but really to take the boat to

Liverpool, my schoolbag packed with clothes, my savings in the pocket of my gymslip.

Searching for Asylum in a sprawling city full of nightclubs, bars and discos was impossible without an address. The landlady in the bed and breakfast I booked into did her best to help by making inquiries, phoning around various venues. After a few days, when I hadn't found them and my money was running out, she advised me to go home. When she said, "Your family will be frantic," I thought of my mother's anxious face and left.

At home I let them rant and rave until their curiosity died down when they realised I wasn't going to tell them anything. In the crowded classroom I sat silently by the window waiting for the whispered innuendoes, the nudges and winks, to subside. I felt older than my classmates now, streetwise. It was all ahead of them. One day they would learn that the fellas they talked about endlessly, dressed up for, pinned all their hopes and dreams on, could mess up their lives so easily.

I returned to work in Eddie Rocket's on Saturdays. Outside, after work, I would find myself looking among the shoppers for a glimpse of Adam. Sometimes, walking home, I would imagine I saw him ahead of me, his long hair flying in the wind, his confident stride, his gorgeous smile. Once I ran after him, calling his name, but it wasn't him. I had to stop and take a deep breath and make myself realise that it never would be him.

Nearly a year had passed and I was stacking dishes in the wash-up when Tracy came in and whispered in my ear "You've got a visitor."

"Who?"

"Him."

"Oh, God." I could feel the blood rush to my face and my stomach churn as I yanked off my rubber gloves and, smoothing my hair, walked outside.

Mark McEvoy, eighteen, a singer with Breaking Glass,

the band we'd joined for the summer, was standing at the counter wearing his biker's leathers, a red scarf blazing around his neck.

"Hi." He smiled at me. "You finished yet?"

"Almost."

Tracy was clearing the last table, watching from her corner.

"Coming for a spin?" he asked.

"I'd love to." I glanced helplessly at Tracy, whose averted face hid a smile.

"Won't be a minute," I said, turning and walking quickly to the kitchen, tearing off my apron and cap as I went, afraid he might not wait for me.

"That him?" Tracy swung through the door, balancing the heavy tray precariously before setting it down.

"Yes." I yanked my bag from the hook behind the door, making for the cloakroom. "Isn't he gorgeous?"

She followed me.

"Thanks, Tracy. You're an angel. I'll work extra tomorrow," I said, pulling my hairbrush from my bag.

"No need. Listen, Becky, do you know what you're doing?"

The brush tore through my hair. I stared at her.

"I like him, if that's what you mean."

"He's from our road. You could be out of your depth here," she said.

"I can take care of myself." I snatched my bag and made for the door.

"See you tomorrow!" I called over my shoulder.

"It's your business. Don't say I didn't warn you."

I was out the door, free, running without looking back.

"I didn't think you'd turn up," I said as nonchalantly as I could, climbing on to his motorcycle behind him.

"I couldn't wait," he laughed.

We took off down the road swaying with the curves and dips, rushing past the green blur of trees and hedgerows, the wind in our ears, the blue patch of sky widening at the horizon, hope in the rest of the day.

DAMSON JAM

Siobhán Parkinson

"Made to an authentic recipe," announced the label on the mustard pot. Well, what *other* sort of recipe could there be? A *fake* recipe? A recipe that isn't a recipe at all, but is really a bus ticket in disguise, or the plans for a nuclear power station cleverly encoded to *look* like a mustard recipe? I looked inside the mustard pot. It was full of tiny brown and tan ball-bearings suspended in a thick and evil-looking yellow paste. Very suspicious.

"It's amazing," I muttered, meaning how they had got the nuclear power station into a little jar like that.

"'Snot mayonnaise," said my sister Carla, who was slightly deaf that week because she had a cold, and who had apparently been sitting on the other side of the breakfast table all along, eating her toast and *watching* me and *listening* to my private thoughts. "'Smustard," she offered, by way of clarification.

Her name's not really Carla. It's Caroline. But she was going through one of her phrases, as my mum wittily calls it. The previous month it had been ironing the creases out of her jeans. That I can sympathise with, up to a point. My mum just cannot get it into her head that carefully ironed-in creases are naff in jeans. But not naff enough to be worth the trouble of actually ironing them out again, unless you're Caroli . . . I mean Carla.

I didn't explain to her about the mustard recipe. She wouldn't understand. She'd say it was me being *literal* again. She makes being literal sound like the Eighth Deadly Sin. Anyway, I'm not. I just like to be *accurate*.

"Colman!" Carla suddenly shrieked.

I hasten to add that she did not mean me. My name is Cornelius. You may laugh, but it's an old and very respectable family name. And it is not as bad as Colman. Anyway, I'm called Con for short.

I am an astute and observant brother, so I knew what Caroline meant. The mustard had given her an idea for a name for the baby. It's a sort of family joke by now. My other sister is called Carina. Get it? I don't think my parents really intended to call all their children by names beginning with C. It just sort of crept up on them, but now that there are three of us, it would be a shame to break the tradition, or that's how Carla argues anyway.

Not that there is much danger of that. My mother isn't even *pregnant,* for God's sake, but Carla says it's best to be prepared and women of her age do the oddest things. You can gather that she (Carla, I mean) is neurotic. My mother isn't *that* odd, in spite of the business with the jeans, but Carla has lists of names beginning with C stuck up all over the house, just in case.

Carla had found her schoolbag by now and was stomping up and down the hall shouting for her camogie stick. She's always losing it, and she seems to think that marching up and down shouting for it is going to make it appear, as if it were a little dog.

"Oh my God!" she yelled. She'd appeared back at the door. Calling the camogie stick seemed to have worked, because she was brandishing it like a weapon of war. "We probably can't ask her to the *christening*!" And she cut a slice out of the air with her samurai-camogie stick.

"Who?" I asked, screwing the lid back on the mustard. I didn't bother to ask her whose christening. Colman's evidently. Poor little sausage. Hadn't even been conceived, and Carla had decided not only his sex and name, but who was on the invitation list to his christening. I thought of suggesting she should take out an education policy now and maybe give Brown Thomas's a ring and tell them to stand by for the wedding-present list.

"Eleanor," she said impatiently.

"Eleanor?"

"Elinora, Evelina, Angelina, Alannah, whatever her name is."

"Oh, you mean *Alison*," I said.

"That's what I said, Alison. Anyway, you can see how dreadful it would be. She mightn't know what to *do*. She probably doesn't even know how to bless herself. She'd probably die of *embarrassment*. Oh, the poor girl!"

She spun on her heel and plunged back through the hall and out the door, to school. I packed my lunch into my schoolbag, also Carla's lunch, which she'd left in the fridge, and followed her at a safe distance. I didn't want any more projections about how embarrassed Alison might be at a hypothetical christening for a non-existent baby.

Alison exists OK. And I have actually *met* her, which is more than enough for Carla to build not only a romance on but an engagement, a marriage, a family, maybe even a divorce – if she could just get over the hurdle of the patent impossibility of involving Alison in anything even remotely involving religious ritual.

Alison, I must explain, is a Protestant. Carla says their names are a giveaway. She's not the horsey sort, but you can tell all the same, because she has those high cheekbones and that sort of *strained* look they all have. It's sexy, in a weird way. Her skin is sort of translucent. You can see the veins through it, which sounds gross and yicky, but isn't. Also, she has a smashing figure, but I don't think that's got anything to do with her religion. It's funny that they send her to the convent, but Carla says it's dead posh these days to have a convent education, and that our school wouldn't be good enough for her, even though it's non-denom (in theory).

I was mulling all this over as I kicked my way to school. It's a habit I've got into, walking in the gutter and kicking the kerb with the side of my shoe. My left shoe is all scuffed on one side from doing that. Carla says I should do it on the way home as well, to balance things out, but I keep forgetting.

Anyway, there I was, scuffling and kicking and wondering whether Alison's mother makes damson jam – my Uncle Jim says all Protestants do – when I heard a voice calling "Hi, Con!" A light, musical voice.

Alison!

I looked up. She was gliding towards me on a bicycle. She was wearing that horrible green thing they make them wear at that school she goes to, but she still looked like a . . . well, I'm not one for poetry, but let's say she didn't look as if she could ever do anything as mundane as make damson jam. (Which reminds me, what the hell are damsons anyway?) She skated gracefully to a halt and put one dainty foot on the road to balance herself. Then she slithered off the saddle and hung over the handlebars to talk to me, looking up at me through her pale fringe.

"Oh, hi!" I said, trying to lower my voice a tone or two, because it is still inclined to squeak a bit, if I'm under pressure.

I wondered if I should ask her out, now that I had her all to myself, but I couldn't think of a single place to ask her, except to Colman's christening. Luckily, I had the presence of mind not to do *that,* but the effort of not doing it had the effect of blotting out every other thing I might say to her, so I just stood there like an idiot, grinning at her, until at last she said, "Well, I'd better be off. Don't want to be late for school."

"Yeh," I grinned. Damn Carla and her fantasies, I thought, coming between me and a golden opportunity like this. "Better get on yer bike, heh?"

"What? Oh yeh, joke, hey, yeh, funny, ha-ha!" she said.

OK, so it was a feeble joke, but hell, I was taken unawares, and my insides were wobbling. It was a miracle I was able to talk at all, much less make sense.

"Well, bye so," I said, and stood up onto the pavement to make myself a bit taller. Not that I'm short or anything, and anyway I'm still growing.

"Come to tea," she shouted back over her shoulder as she sailed off. "My mother's baked a cake."

"Ehh, lovely, cake, yummy," I yelled at her retreating back.

Tea? Oh lord, tea! With her mother! It wasn't exactly my idea of a date. It was like something out of Jane *Austen,* for God's sake.

Anyway, what did *tea* mean? In our house it means a meal with a knife and fork at six o'clock. But did she mean the other kind – tea and cake on china plates at four? It sounded like that kind, because of the cake, but it mightn't be, because obviously you can have cake for the other kind too, after the knife-and-fork course. Life is so *complicated.*

I had to go to Carla's class at lunchtime, because I had her lunchbox. She fell on it as usual and she fell on me too, in gratitude for having remembered it. I thought I'd take advantage of having her in grateful mode and asked her what she thought about the tea problem.

"She's asked you to *tea!*" she yelped. *"Tea!"*

"Keep your voice down, Caroline," I said between gritted teeth. "The whole of Transition doesn't need to know about it. Carla, I mean."

"Yes, but tea is so . . . *intimate*!" Carla said in a stage whisper. She made it sound like risqué underwear.

I blushed. I'm working on not minding about blushing, but it's difficult. Not that I do it all that much, but you have to admit that a word like "intimate" is a bit embarrassing in mixed company, even if it's only your sister.

"What do you mean?" I sputtered. "How could it be?"

"Well, I mean sort of, oh . . . *pointed*," said Carla, unhelpfully. "It means introducing you to her *mother.* Doesn't that sound as if she's *serious,* to you? Before you know where you are she'll be asking Dad for your *hand.* Lord, *how* are we going to handle the christening? Suppose she does a solo with the frilly bit at the end of the Our Father."

"Carla, you are being ridiculous," I said. Actually, I think I'll get a recording made of that sentence and just *give* it to Carla. It would save me a lot of vocal effort.

"It's not ridiculous. They *do* add a frilly bit."

"I don't mean that. I mean . . . oh, Carla, you are so *absurd!*" I said in exasperation. There was no point in even starting to list her absurdities.

"I thought of Crispin," Carla answered, vaguely. "But do you think a boy called Crispin would get bullied at school?"

I was tempted to ask how she was so certain it was going to be a boy, but I realised just in time that if I said that, it meant I'd conceded there really *was* going to be a baby.

"Anyway, would you think she meant the four o'clock kind of tea?"

"Indubitably," said Carla. It's one of her words-of-the-week. "She couldn't ask you to the other kind on the spur of the moment. She'd have to check with her mum. I'd say be there for four. Or half past."

As it turned out, it wasn't a bit Jane Austen. She had just meant what my mum calls "a cup of tea in your hand". A normal person would have said "call around after school", not "come to tea", but there, you see, you have to make allowances for cultural differences.

There *was* cake. Really cool cake, with walnuts. And her mum breezed in for a minute to say she was going out for firelighters, but she just nodded at me, didn't even ask my name. I remembered to stand up when she came into the room. She had one of those wicker baskets over her arm, like Red Riding Hood. I began to see what Carla meant about the frilly bit on the end of the Our Father. She wore men's shoes, with laces. She could easily embarrass a person at a christening.

When she left, we went into the living-room and played

some smoochy music. We didn't quite get as far as doing what smoochy music was invented for, but I had the distinct impression that we made a good start.

Carla met me at the door when I got home. She was breathless with excitement. So was I, but of another kind.

"Guess what?" she demanded.

"Tell me," I said wearily.

"No, no, guess!"

"They've discovered life on Mars?" I ventured.

"Don't be so out*land*ish," said Carla. "Guess again."

"The parish priest's run off with a flower-seller," I tried.

"Now you are just being offensive," she said primly.

"How did you know I meant a *male* flower-seller?" I asked.

"Really?" said Carla, her eyes widening. You can't afford to joke with Carla. She is not very aware of the line between fact and fantasy. "I didn't know you could specialise like that."

"Specialise?"

"In male flowers," she explained. "Anyway, that's not the point, the point is, it's a girl."

"What is?"

"*Who* is, you mean," said Carla. "The baby. It's a *girl*."

"*What* baby?" I asked, bewildered. Surely she couldn't have *willed* this wretched child into being?

"Oh, sorry, I forgot. Well, you know all these names I've been picking for babies? Just in case? Sort of wishful thinking?"

"Ye-es," I said, dreading what was coming next. My Airfix collection suddenly looked as if it might be in mortal danger. And after I'd just got my bedroom looking the way I want, with the Subbuteo pitch just in the very middle. Maybe they'd make me move out and give that room to the girls, if there were going to be three of them. They'd coveted it for years.

"Well," she said triumphantly, "it seems to have sort of rubbed off. Only not on Mum. It's Aunt Ellen. She had a scan and they made a mistake at the clinic and told her it was a girl, even though she didn't want to know, and she said that if she knows we may as well all know, and isn't that *wonderful*?"

Aunt Ellen has been dying to have a baby for ages, so it *was* rather wonderful, I suppose.

"Does that make me an uncle?" I asked, trying not to sound too relieved about the Subbuteo pitch.

"No, silly, a cousin."

"Is *that* all?"

I'm that already. It didn't seem adequate, somehow, to the occasion. After all, Carla practically *conjured* this baby out of thin air. You have to hand it to her. She's very creative.

"What about Claudia?" asked Carla, cutting the bread for tea.

"Mmm," said Mum non-committally. "I think Ellen is thinking of Mary Rose."

"That'll do," conceded Carla. "Claudia Mary is very elegant, isn't it, Con?"

I sighed.

"I'm going to be the godmother!" Carla said then. "Did you know?"

Carina, whose face was full of sausage at this stage, shook her head and my mother looked at Carla suspiciously. There is no way of telling when Carla is making stuff up. She doesn't really understand the difference, you see.

"I think we could have Aileen at the christening after all, Con," Carla conceded.

"Alison," I muttered.

"Yes. I mean, after all, she's a Christian," she said piously, "and that's what it's all *about*, isn't it Mum?"

My mother ignored her. She knows better than to engage with Carla when she's all wound up like that.

I managed to escape to my room soon afterwards. I explained that I didn't feel like much tea, as I'd had some already. My mother gave me one of those remote I'd-like-to-take-your-temperature looks, but I outstared her and hoofed it off up the stairs to the sanctity of my room, where I threw myself on my bed and thought about . . . well, it wasn't damsons anyway. Let's say that a small smile played about my lips.

The baby got born, but he turned out to be a Colman after

all, or a Crispin. Fat lot of good those scans are if they can't get a simple thing like that right. Aunt Ellen got a proper shock, but she made the best of it, or that's how she put it anyway, which I have to say I thought was just a touch sexist. And of course she didn't call him any of those names. She called him Simon. Carla swallowed her disappointment and said that Simon was a lovely name, although personally she preferred Christopher, but then it wasn't her baby.

"Let's be thankful for small mercies," I heard my mother say under her breath. I'm afraid Carla is a bit of a trial to my mother at the moment.

And Alison came to the christening. Well, at this stage, we've been going out – or more accurately, staying in – for a good seven months. And of *course* she didn't do anything embarrassing.

The only really embarrassing moment happened about six months ago, when I met her coming out of the church one Sunday morning. Our church, I mean. I was going in to the half eleven and she was coming out of the half ten.

"Oh!" I said. "You've been to Mass?"

"It's *Sunday*," she said, as if that was enough of an explanation, dipping her finger in the holy-water font and blessing herself solemnly. Then she leaned towards me and planted her middle finger, still damp from the holy water, on my forehead. My whole body seemed to shrink to that one little moist fingerprint.

"See you tomorrow," she whispered, and then she was gone.

I stared after her. In spite of the magic imprint of her finger, still palpitating on my forehead, at that moment Alison lost just a teeny bit of that shimmer she had seemed, until then, to move in. Not that she is any the less wonderful for just being one of ourselves. It's not that. I can't explain it really. It's like she'd lost some of her mystique or something. I know it's a bit stupid really.

I suppose I never *will* get to find out about damson jam now.

FIRST MEAT

Tom Richards

I didn't want to go to Vietnam. Not at the end of 1972, I didn't. I was eighteen years old. Ripe meat for the draft. By then, the thinking population of the United States had realised that it was a stupid war. Every night on the CBS Evening News, Walter Cronkite – a news reader that most Americans trusted like Jesus Christ – gave us the day's scoreboard.

It read like a college basketball game. Americans: 57 killed, 126 wounded. Estimated Viet Cong count: 269 killed, and God alone knew how many wounded.

Not that God had anything to do with it.

All wars are stupid, of course. But this one sat in the American people's craw like an undiagnosed cancer.

At the beginning of the Vietnam conflict – back in '66 and '67 – most of us so-called fresh-blooded American males wanted to get out there to prove ourselves. Be a hero. Be a man. Be a something.

President Johnson, and then President Nixon, told us that it was a moral imperative. Whatever the hell that was. But we bought it. We wanted to go, all of us. We let the politicians drive us forward toward the promise of a stinking precipice that none of us understood.

In 1968 – I was fourteen – we played Vietnam just like we had played cowboys and Indians in our earlier days. We memorised the hardware and the language like budding military tacticians. We chased each other around the fields of my parents' farm, bayoneting each other in rituals of imaginary blood-letting. And all around the cattle grazed, gazing at us with knowing eyes.

They understood blood-letting.

Sometimes, my father would call for me. We'd take a truck full of cattle down to the mart. I'd watch as the beasts were driven into the pens, their breath blowing white in the cold Nebraska autumn. Then we'd drive home again and in the wind-blown grass of the empty fields I'd play Vietnam with my friends.

We were the good guys. Charlie was the bad guy. It was as black and white as a 1960 Superman flick. When we were finished playing we'd go home to thick sandwiches of peanut butter and jam and tall glasses of ice-cold milk. Our mothers would stand over us, comforted in the knowledge that we were safe.

But then the war started to go wrong. Each night Walter Cronkite brought another slaughterhouse of death into our homes. The bloody bodies of America's sons were paraded across the television screens like a technicolour meat market. An uneasiness settled across the rolling prairies of America, spreading even into the Nebraska fields.

In Chicago war protestors were attacked by policemen at the Democratic National Convention. On college campuses the protests started. At Kent State University students were murdered by the National Guard.

Our black and white certainty had been replaced by the grey shadows of fear and betrayal. Our mothers still stood behind us but now their worried hands clutched our shoulders, wondering if their son would be the next sacrifice.

And at night I dreamed of cattle waiting for the slaughter.

In 1972, when I was eighteen and eligible for the draft, the killing fields of Vietnam were still bathed in blood. Men died and had to be replaced. Despite the protests, despite the stink that had entered the moral conscience, the military still called up replacements. The draft still dealt its deadly hand.

And for guys like me the game that we called Vietnam was about to become real.

"Your first mission?" he shouted above the howling turbines.

"Yeah," I said.

Lieutenant Jesse Wilson smiled all the way to his sunset eyes. He reminded me of a cowboy in search of his herd. His weathered face and hands looked as if they had rustled a thousand bucking broncos. He chewed on a ball of gum and I guessed that he would have much preferred a wad of tobacco.

He stared levelly at me, as if trying to figure out if I was going to be a troublesome stallion or only a frightened mare. He seemed to come to a decision on that point. He spat on to the tarmac and chewed on his gum some more.

"You just keep close to me, Johnson. It's all going to work out fine."

Then he loped across the airport tarmac toward the waiting helicopter. I didn't know what else to do so I followed him.

I was at a military airbase located just north of Saigon. As I ran across the concrete paving my flight boots felt as heavy as death. I had only been in Nam for three days. Already I hated it.

We ran past a C130 Hercules cargo plane. Soldiers were lifting body bags, running them double-time up the ramp and into the darkened belly of the aircraft. To me the body bags looked like dark carcasses ready for processing. I had to wonder if soon I wouldn't be among them.

This was Vietnam. I could smell it. Taste it. Feel it. This was no game.

Our helicopter was right in front of us. I watched while Wilson climbed into the right seat, as if mounting his horse. Behind him the gunners were already in position. They grasped their 50-calibre machine guns in sweating hands. I stood on the tarmac staring at them. Wilson yelled at me impatiently.

"Johnson, for God's sakes, don't just stand there. Get into the aircraft."

I opened the left hand door and climbed into the co-pilot's seat. Wilson was already caressing the controls. Behind me I could hear the jet turbines light, their throaty roar whistling upward into a scream. Wilson engaged the rotors. Above me, the two-bladed prop cut into the humid air.

Wilson looked at me and I thought I could detect pity in his sky-blue eyes. He nodded. "Don't you worry, son. You just let old Wilson do the worrying."

Wilson winked, then grasped the collective with his left hand and gunned the throttle. The Huey shuddered and we pulled up from the hot concrete of the airbase. Below us, I could see the green forests of Vietnam spread out in the sunlight.

Green forests of hope, I thought. But I knew that shrouded within their shadows waited the reality of the game that I now played for the first time.

We headed north. Wilson turned and introduced me to the rest of the crew.

"Bill Johnson, meet Henry James." I looked over my shoulder. A big black man with a face like a prize Angus steer grinned back at me. He looked nervous and I could see ice-cold sweat drip from his meaty chin. I tried to smile at him through my fear.

"And this is Boy Friday," Wilson said. The soldier at the other machine gun nodded at me. He looked even younger than I was. What caught me most about Friday were his eyes. As dark and as sad as the beasts which my father and I took to the mart.

"Boy Friday got his nick-name because he's always hoping that tomorrow's the week-end, and he gets to go home. Ain't that right, Friday?" Wilson said, smiling at him.

Friday only nodded.

"Did ya' get a letter from that girl of yours, Friday?" Wilson asked. He was trying to take the edge off a situation which was as sharp as a butcher's knife. Friday nodded and tapped his flak jacket. I could imagine the simple words of love and loneliness sent from a far away sweetheart buried beneath the thick material.

"You keep that letter close to you, Friday," Wilson said. "Someday soon you'll get to touch the hand that wrote it. I promise." Friday didn't say anything.

"You hear me, Friday?" Wilson stated again. "I promise."

Boy Friday looked at him for a long moment, then nodded again. He didn't say anything because he was scared to believe the lieutenant. In fact, nobody said much on that first mission. Only our fear talked.

But Wilson kept on talking. He chattered and whooped and laughed as he drove our reluctance into unknown territory.

He joked with us for a quick five minutes. Then he gave us the mission plan. He was as straight and as honest as he knew how. "Got a little trouble up north of here, boys."

"How far north?"

"About a hundred and forty clicks," Wilson answered. His voice was light, but filled with unstated worry.

"Charlie's active as hell up there," Henry James said. I turned and looked at him. Henry's eyes had rolled upward, and the whites of those eyes smelled of fear.

Wilson grinned, trying to make light of it. "You know it, son. We got a platoon surrounded up there. They've taken some casualties. They need a little support. Just like a goddam military jock strap." He slapped me on the thigh. "You boys just let Wilson take care of it. You'll get back to base. Guaranteed."

Then he went back to his flying. His weathered hands gripped the controls surely as he rode the big Huey north. But as we choppered over the dense vegetation I wondered if this first mission was also to be my last.

We put down in some godforsaken field. The blast from the rotor kicked up a hurricane of dust. I couldn't see much. Then the dust cleared. A half-mile away a burned-out village smoked. The field was pitted from mortar shell fire.

Wilson shut down the engine. A jeep pulled up in front of us. An officer stepped on to the broken field. Wilson nodded to him, then turned to us. "Take five, gentlemen. The area is secure. Wander up to that village if you've a mind to." He pointed to the officer. "Just give me a few minutes with the Captain here."

"You sure it's secure, Lieutenant?" Henry James asked.

"Got my word on it, son," Wilson said. "You think I'd put you down in a hot spot just for some Texan jaw?" He smiled and James relaxed. "Now go on and get outa' here."

The three of us looked at him. When Wilson smiled, there was something about him that I trusted. As if he were a saint or Houdini or the local policeman back home. He had said that it was safe. We believed him.

Wilson got out of the chopper and wandered over to the Army officer. His back was to us as he talked and I could see the broken lines on his neck, as weathered as old leather.

We struck out toward the village. The war that Walter Cronkite reported into my living room now surrounded me like a coming darkness. It had little to do with the games that I had played as a kid.

The village was gutted. The grass huts had been burned. An ox lay butchered, its body bloated in the sun. The stench was nauseating.

"God in Heaven," Friday whispered.

The villagers who had not escaped lay stretched out on a shattered piece of ground. No one had thought to cover them. We walked past the torn bodies as if we were walking past a butcher's window. Old men and young women lay there. Heads crushed. Entrails covered with flies. Young girls sprawled, naked, their legs spread. Brown eyes gazed up at me, soft innocent looks that tore through my stomach like cold knives.

"Who did this?" I whispered.

"Don't make no difference," Henry James breathed. "They're dead. Makes no difference who did it."

Then Friday sucked his breath in quick. He shied like a frightened beast and I pulled my side-arm. Friday stared down at something that lay in the grass. I moved toward it. An earthen-coloured blanket covered a gentle hump. I pulled it aside, regretting instantly that I had done so.

A five-month-old baby lay nestled at her mother's exposed breast, as if she was suckling. But the blood that still swam from the shattered body meant that she suckled no more.

"Oh my God oh my God oh my God."

Friday buckled, spewing vomit on to the dry earth. Then he bolted. He ran back toward the safety of the chopper.

I stared at the child. This was no game. Not that it had ever been one. Henry James and I reached out and touched each other, wanting to feel the warmth of the living. Then we turned and stumbled back toward the chopper and Wilson.

Wilson was already sitting in the Huey. When I saw him, I felt like I was seeing my own father.

"Lock 'n load! Five minutes out, gentlemen."

Wilson's command was greeted with silence. He turned in his seat. "Friday? Henry James? Where you boys gone to?"

I looked in the back. Both of them sat huddled next to their machine guns. Below us, Vietnam sped beneath the belly of our helicopter.

"You boys all right?" Wilson asked.

Friday started to sob. His cries were cut up by the mechanical thrash of our turbines. Friday's body rocked to a rhythm of grief which he alone could hear.

Wilson's eyes were tired, as if he had seen this a

thousand times before. "Johnson, you fly for awhile. I'm going back to talk to Friday."

I took the controls. Wilson unbuckled and crawled into the back. Through my earphones, I could hear his words of comfort.

He reminded me of my father, comforting the beasts on their way to the cattle mart.

I looked down at the jungle. It was getting dark. Wilson sat next to me. He was flying again. Behind us, Friday and Henry James crouched beside their guns. Friday had stopped crying. But his eyes stared huge from his boy's face. He was still shaken. In his hand he clutched the letter from his girl.

The side doors of the chopper were open and the wind howled into the cabin. Henry James scanned the forest, looking for Charlie. His eyes were bright with fear.

"This here's going to be a regular Sunday afternoon trip to Grandma's," Wilson said . . . his voice floated toward us like a preacher's . . . "Guaranteed." He grinned at me. The sweat underneath my flight helmet felt like warm urine.

"You're from Nebraska, ain't you, Johnson?" he asked me. He was trying to keep me from thinking of what lay ahead, just as my father had tried to keep me from remembering the final destination of the doomed cattle.

"Yes, sir. Just north of Grand Island."

"Pretty country," he said, and I knew that he had been there.

"My father's got a farm out there. We raise beef and dairy cattle."

"Ah-huh," he nodded. "Thought so. I can tell a rancher when I see one. Been messing with cattle and horses most of my days, myself. Shuffling beasts from one end of Texas to the other. Never lost one yet." His leather face glistened in the dying rays of the sun. "Don't worry, Johnson. You'll see it all again. Promise."

I tried hard to believe him. He grinned at me, and I hoped to God that he spoke the truth.

"Smoke!"

I looked down. A smoke marker spread an angry red pall over the forest. "That'll be our platoon, gentlemen. Looking for a ride home. You-all just keep your eyes peeled for Charlie. I'll do the rest."

Wilson turned the chopper as if spinning a champion stallion and began his descent into a small clearing.

Then things started to happen quick.

A line of American troops streamed out of the forest's edge. There must have been fifteen of them. Three of them were wounded, carried by their buddies.

I looked over at Wilson. His mouth was set tight. He shook his head.

"Too many of 'em, goddammit! Too many of 'em."

We were ten feet off the ground when the forest erupted with small arms fire.

"Charlie!" Friday shouted.

Both 50s opened up. The Huey vibrated, spent shell-casing clattering to the metal floor. Wilson dropped the chopper toward the ground. The platoon had hit the deck. They lay in the long grass. More firing . . . slugs reaching out, trying to touch them – us – with their finality. The chopper shuddered; I heard tearing metal, hoping to God that nothing vital was hit. Hoping to God that we would get out of this.

Friday and Henry James were screaming into their microphones. Their terror filled my head. "Three o'clock! Nail the bastards!" . . . a machine gun chattered. Foliage ripped into tiny patterns of drifting green. "In those trees! Throw some in there!" The guns spoke again.

The chopper touched down. The platoon leader put his arm up. The platoon rose as one, terrified sons trying to go home. Wilson's eyes watched them carefully. Behind us the machine guns spat out death, covering them as they sprinted toward us.

The first of the platoon was clambering aboard the chopper when Wilson saw a youngster catch a round in the leg. He went down hard.

Wilson popped his door. He turned to me. "You stay here," he yelled. "I'm going to get that kid."

My feet were frozen to the floor. I knew that I should follow; wanted to follow. Not able to. "You sure, Lieutenant?"

He smiled at me. Then he was out of the chopper, running toward the wounded soldier.

Most of the platoon was in the Huey, now. The cabin was as crowded as a cattle pen. I looked back quick. Friday and Henry James had their guns firing, trying to cover Wilson. I watched as he ran toward the wounded man, helping him up. Running him awkwardly back toward the aircraft . . .

. . . taking a Vietnamese round in the shoulder . . . staggering hard. Picking himself up again, then the boy. Moving in slow motion toward us . . .

. . . handing the soldier into the chopper and looking, finally, at me.

I could see the blood on his fatigues; on his face. He reached in, grabbing a semi-automatic rifle, pulling it away from the Huey in one fluid motion.

"Johnson! You get this thing up in the air NOW! You hear that, boy?"

I couldn't, I wouldn't believe his words. He was wounded, but not critically. He would make it. We would all make it. That's what he had promised us.

"Lieutenant, get in here. Get in now, for God's sake."

Through the smoke and the chatter of gun-fire, I could see his eyes study me. The far away look of a cowboy seeing the trail's end was in them. Wilson reached out and grasped my shoulder. He smiled and for a moment that was all there was. Just his smile.

Then he leaned toward me, making sure that I could hear

him over the gun-fire. "We're too heavy as it is. Now, fly on out of here and get these people home."

"For God's sake, Lieutenant . . ."

His eyes quieted me.

"I promised."

That's all he said.

I didn't know what I felt. Knowing he was right. Knowing that we were already at our weight limit. Not knowing what else to do. I heard the firing again and Friday was screaming like a stuck pig, yelling that he'd been hit. Wilson's hand tightened on my shoulder, then withdrew. I watched his steady eyes and that smile of his. Then my hand reached out, as if it was his own, and grasped the throttle.

We rose from the field, away from him, in a volley of enemy fire. He gazed up at me, his face still smiling. My eyes never left Lieutenant Jesse Wilson until we turned and he fell from view, lost in the smoke and gunfire of the firestorm below us.

In the years since the end of Vietnam I often wander out on to the open fields where we played our games and watch the cattle as they feed at pasture. Now and then I still wake in the night, remembering that first mission.

My own children play war games now, for such is the circle of things. They run through the wind-swept fields screaming in their innocence. But long after their laughter dies I sit alone in the grass and think back on a place and time where reality became more than a game.

The America that I knew is long dead. But certain things do not die. In Vietnam, I first came to understand the warmth of a smile. I first came to understand the real meaning of a promise.

It burns like a flame within my heart and will not soon be extinguished.

NO ONE UNDERSTANDS

Marilyn Taylor

"He's coming back." Mum's words hit Claire like a bombshell. "He wants to see you both."

Claire gazed, speechless, at the letter in Mum's hand.

"That's brill," said her younger sister Michelle, slurping up her Frosties. "I hope he gets here before my birthday."

"Don't be stupid," said Claire sharply. "There's no way he's suddenly going to remember your birthday after four years."

"Well, he writes to us sometimes, doesn't he?" retorted Michelle. "And he sends money."

"Who wants his bleeding money?" said Claire. She stared down at her untouched bowl of cereal, her thin face pinched in a frown.

Mum, pale and washed-out without her make-up, sat nervously folding and unfolding the letter. In the background the radio chattered away to itself, unheeded.

Waves of alarm spread through Claire like the ripples from a stone thrown into water. Why did he want to see them after all this time? They were doing all right without him. Why couldn't he leave them in peace?

Unwelcome memories from the past sprang into her mind. The raised voices late at night; her mother sobbing as she crept upstairs, quietly, so as not to wake them; the slam of the front door. In the morning, the bitter silence as they all ate breakfast, her father hidden behind the paper. And the relief when she got to school, away from it all.

There had only been one person she could talk to, and that was Sam, who lived two doors down from them. He wasn't really a boyfriend, more like a brother, but nicer and more caring than most brothers. She could tell Sam anything. He'd helped her through the awful time when Dad had finally left, his suitcase hastily packed, his face rigid as he gave her and Michelle a peck on the cheek, all of them trying not to hear the sounds from above of Mum crying.

And then he was gone, far away, leaving a void in all their lives.

Claire's thoughts came back to the present. Her mother, shoulders hunched in her worn track-suit top, stood watching the rain streaming down the kitchen window. After a moment she turned round. With an effort she asked Claire, "Tuna OK for your sandwiches?"

There was a silence. Then Claire burst out, "I won't see him."

Mum said slowly, "Claire, he's still your father." She paused, and added, "But, of course, it's your decision."

Michelle jumped up from the table, her round pretty face, framed by a mass of curly hair, bright with anticipation. "Well, *I* can't wait to see him again," she said. "I bet he'll bring us great presents. Do they have roller blades in Saudi Arabia?"

At lunchtime Claire sat alone in a corner of the school canteen eating her sandwiches, a book propped in front of her so she wouldn't have to talk to anyone. She could see Michelle, as usual at the centre of an eager crowd, enthusiastically regaling them with the news about Dad.

Two girls sat down at Claire's table. Ignoring her frown one of them asked, "Is it true your Dad's coming back to Ireland and he's stinking rich and you're all going to move to a huge house and your sister's getting six pairs of designer jeans and a new stereo?"

Claire glared at them. "Just piss off, will you?"

"No wonder she's got no friends," one of them said to the other as they flounced off.

Clare heaved a sigh. She knew the incident wasn't going to boost her popularity in school, which was already zilch. Unlike Michelle, Claire had never been able to chat easily about boys and clothes and TV soaps, or to laugh and giggle and complain about nothing in particular. And since Dad's departure she'd withdrawn more and more into herself, unable to confide in the few friends she had.

Except Sam.

The bell went for class. Slowly, Claire gathered her books together and slung her bag over her shoulder. After tea that evening, she'd call in to Sam and tell him the news. Only he knew how confused she'd felt after her father left – her relief at the peace after so much tension and anger; her bitterness towards Dad for starting a new life without them; the irritation mixed with pity she had felt each day when she came home from school to find her mother red-eyed and silent, the dirty breakfast dishes still piled in the sink.

Sam would understand how she felt about this new bombshell.

Sam's house was always warm and noisy with lots of things happening. Sam's mother welcomed Claire with a smile and explained she was rushing off to her yoga class. Sam's dad was in the kitchen cooking a Chinese meal and there were sounds of rock music and computer games from all over the house.

Up in his room Sam was sprawled on the duvet strumming his guitar, oblivious to all that was going on around him. Claire's heart lurched with pleasure when she saw him, cuddly in his huge woolly sweatshirt like a friendly bear.

He grinned as she came in. But when he saw her expression he put down the guitar, jumped off the bed and came over to her.

"What's up, Claire?" he asked, looking down at her, his brown eyes gentle.

When she said nothing he bent down and gave her a big hug. Burying her head in his blue sweatshirt, smelling his familiar smell, she felt safe and protected, his encircling arms shutting out all her problems.

After a moment he said, "Come on, let's go for a walk down by the river."

Claire followed him downstairs and out into the mild spring evening. The rain had stopped, and the front garden was scattered with fallen blossom, like pink confetti.

Sam whistled as they set off, and his spaniel Bono came flying after them, his long ears flapping as he jumped up on them barking expectantly and trying to lick their faces.

Claire and Sam sauntered along the path to where the grassy riverbank opened out into their special secret place. It was almost hidden by weeping willows, their new leaves a shining silvery-green. Sam threw a stick and Bono leaped joyfully after it into the rushing water. When he scrambled out he shook himself, splattering them with glittering droplets.

Sitting on the trunk of a fallen tree Claire told Sam the news.

"I hate him, Sam," she said. "I can't forget what he did to us." She paused, gripping her hands together tightly. "After he went away we heard he was living with someone else." Gazing at Sam, willing him to understand, she went on, "I never want to see him again."

After a moment he said, "Of course, you don't *have* to see him." Claire felt a rush of relief. He continued, "But it mightn't have been all his fault. Or your Mum's either." Claire stiffened.

Sam put his hand on hers. "Sometimes these things just happen. It mightn't necessarily be anyone's fault."

"Of course it's someone's fault," she replied sharply.

"He's the one who left." Disappointment washed over her. "You don't understand either, Sam. You're just like all the rest."

"I do understand, Claire," he said. "But he's your dad. I mean, it's natural that he'd want to see you after all this time – "

"I'm going back," she said abruptly. He tried to put his arm round her but she shook him off.

They retraced their steps in a tense silence. Even Bono was subdued, his ears drooping sadly.

As they approached Sam's house Michelle appeared, breathless. "Claire," she called, "Dad's on the phone from Saudi Arabia. I've spoken to him already. Mum says you've to come quick – "

"No," said Claire. "I'm not talking to him."

"But Mum said – "

"Just tell him to get lost," snapped Claire. She watched as Michelle turned back to their house.

A hard knot of misery lay in the pit of Claire's stomach. Sam's face was cold. "You could have at least talked to him," he said, and strode up the path to his house, Bono lolloping obediently after him.

Claire stood there alone, tears of anger and misery trickling down her cheeks. Inside her head a voice whispered, "No one understands."

Claire walked slowly home from school, head down, feeling the soft caress of the rain on her hair. She hadn't heard from Sam for nearly a week now and it felt like a year. He'd called over once, but she'd told her mum to say she had a headache. She really did have one. In fact she seemed to have a constant headache nowadays, but that had never stopped her from seeing Sam before.

Michelle had chattered on incessantly about the phone call. Dad had wanted to know how tall they were, what they were studying, what clothes they liked. He'd told Michelle

146

how much he'd missed them both and that he had their photos beside his bed.

"Please, spare me," Claire had snapped.

"Oh, Claire." Her mum patted her shoulder. "You think everything's either black or white. Life's not always that simple." She put her cheek to Claire's and she felt her mother's soft velvety skin against hers.

Then Claire shrugged her off and turned away.

On the hall table lay a parcel, covered with foreign stamps and postmarks. Claire saw it as she closed the front door. It was addressed to herself and Michelle in Dad's familiar bold hand-writing.

Michelle rushed in. "It's from Dad," she said, excited.

"You don't say," said Claire sourly.

"Mum said I was to wait till you got home," said Michelle. "Can I open it now?"

Claire shrugged. Michelle opened the parcel. Inside were two packages wrapped in thin tissue, labelled with their names. "This one's for you," she said, holding the smaller one out to Claire. Claire looked away.

Michelle ripped open her own package, and gasped as she pulled out a soft gauzy scarf, all misty blues and greens with tiny gold threads running through it, like some exotic butterfly. "Wow," she breathed. "It's gorgeous."

Mum had appeared from the garden. She watched as Michelle threw the scarf over her head and shoulders where it settled softly, transforming her ordinary prettiness into something strange and mysterious.

"Yes," said Mum with a sad little smile that was almost a grimace, "he always knew how to choose presents."

Michelle eyed the other package. "Aren't you going to open it?"

Claire looked at her scornfully. "I don't want any presents from him."

Mum said quietly, "I think you should at least open it, Claire."

Sullenly Claire undid the package, revealing a small white box. Inside, nestling in the red velvet lining, lay a pair of earrings in the shape of crescent moons, made of thin beaten silver. They all gazed at them. Claire had never seen such beautiful earrings.

"Go on, Claire," wheedled Michelle. "Try them on."

For a moment Claire said nothing. Then she took the earrings out of the box, walked over to the rubbish bin, pressed the pedal to open the lid, and dropped them deliberately into the bin.

She pushed past her mother and ran out of the kitchen, up the stairs, and into her room. Slamming the door, she flung herself on the bed and cried with deep tearing sobs that went on and on, as though they would never stop.

For the next few days Claire dragged herself to school and back. She felt her face clenching into a permanent scowl. She barely spoke to anyone and after a while people stopped even trying to talk to her.

One break-time she saw Michelle showing her new scarf to an admiring group. Then they all turned to look at Claire, and she knew Michelle had been telling them about the earrings.

That evening Michelle babbled away through supper as usual, while Claire ate silently, barely tasting the food. When Mum tried to include her in the conversation, asking bright meaningless questions about school, Claire just nodded or shook her head or grunted in reply, until eventually Mum gave up.

When they'd finished supper Mum said in a light, nervous tone, "Your dad phoned today."

Michelle squealed. "When's he coming?"

Mum looked at Claire. "He wants to take you both out

148

for a meal. He thinks it might be easier for you to meet him in a restaurant, at first, anyway – "

At first. Claire's face darkened. "Oh I see," she said. "He thinks he's going to come back and we're all going to carry on as though nothing happened – "

"Claire – "

" – as though he never went off and left us. Everyone knows he was living in Saudi Arabia with some stupid cow – "

"That's enough, Claire," Mum's usually gentle voice was tight and angry. "I don't want to go over all that. It's between your father and me." Her voice shook. "We're talking about now, not then. He wants to see you." She paused, and added carefully, "It's his right."

"And I want to see him," Michelle chimed in. "He's my dad."

"Well, you can go," shouted Claire. "He might have more presents for you."

"Claire, that's uncalled for," said Mum. Michelle wore her wounded look, guaranteed to gain sympathy when Claire attacked her. Mum went on. "He's booked that new Italian restaurant in town for the three of you for Friday evening." She tried to smile. "I hear they do nice pizzas."

Michelle brightened up. "Pizza! Mmm," she said, throwing Claire a triumphant look.

Claire gazed out of her bedroom window. In the distance a lawnmower buzzed, and below, Mum, wearing Dad's gardening gloves, was weeding among the masses of golden daffodils and tall white narcissi.

If she craned her neck Claire could just see the corner of Sam's garden. She felt a stab of unhappiness at the thought of him. She missed him so much. But something stopped her calling to his house in the old, casual way.

And tomorrow they were supposed to meet Dad in the restaurant. Mum had said nothing more to Claire about it.

But to Claire's surprise Michelle had asked Claire if she was coming. "He wants to see both of us, not just me," Michelle had mumbled, almost as if she were appealing to her.

But Claire refused to be persuaded. "He deserted us," she told Michelle. "He rejected us." Michelle gave up.

Claire turned away from the window, trying to fight off the anger and bitterness that surrounded her like a fog. She did her homework mechanically and listened to the radio. Then she rummaged through the drawer in her desk for the latest Oasis CD.

Something crackled among the jumble of cassettes, letters, old birthday cards and other oddments. She drew out a yellowing snapshot, one of the many she had torn down from her wall after Dad had left.

Taken at the beach, it showed a young carefree Dad in an open-necked check shirt, carrying Michelle, plump in a little white sun-bonnet and frilly bathing costume. Claire, her hair cut in a fringe, was solemnly clutching Dad's hand, her other hand raised to shade her eyes from the sun.

A vivid memory of that day shot into Claire's mind. After Mum had taken the photo Claire had run down to the sea. She remembered walking fearlessly into the flashing, rippling wavelets.

She turned round to look back at the beach, staring up at the huge dizzying arc of deep blue sky and brilliant sun. The sky, the sun, the water seemed to spin around. A powerful wave pushed her off balance. She floundered and thrashed, the sand melting away under her feet, her mouth and nose flooded with salty water. Blindly she gasped for air.

Then strong arms lifted her up and out of the sucking water and sand and swung her to safety. It was Dad, and Claire remembered clinging to him for hours afterwards, refusing to let go. So clear was the recollection Claire could almost taste the salt in her throat, and feel the terrified thumping of her heart.

Still holding the photo she lay on her bed and gradually,

as the evening light faded, a rare feeling of tranquillity stole over her.

As though a locked door had been opened, her thoughts carried her back past the dark times, to other earlier memories she had long blotted out. Her dad painstakingly constructing elaborate sand castles with her on the beach, patiently listening to her lines over and over again for the school play, bringing her and Michelle every week to the library and sitting squashed in a tiny chair absorbed in a story about dinosaurs, while they chose their books.

All the years she had been growing up he had been there for them. Then things had gone wrong. But did that mean everything that had gone before counted for nothing?

Claire drifted into a deep sleep, and dreamed of her childhood.

All through the next day snatches of thoughts and memories from the night before floated in and out of Claire's mind.

In school she kept her distance from Michelle, who was chattering to her friends about the coming evening, what she was going to wear, what she was going to say.

"Is your sister really not going?" she heard one of Michelle's friends ask. Michelle made a face. "You know what Claire's like," she said, and they all nodded, commiserating.

Claire walked slowly home from school, alone as usual. When she reached her own house she found herself carrying on past it to Sam's.

"Claire!" his mum greeted her. "Come in. We haven't seen you for ages."

"Is Sam in?"

"He's gone to rehearse with his group. Why don't you come in and wait for him?"

Claire shook her head, forcing a smile.

She walked on down to the river and sat on their tree-trunk, thinking, and listening to the birdsong and the soothing sound of the water.

She was roused by a familiar barking. Bono flung himself on her, slobbering all over her in delight. Sam's tall figure appeared in front of her, and her heart lifted at the sight of him in his faded scruffy jeans, his eyes seeking hers.

"I've missed you," he said, reaching for her hand.

For a moment Claire couldn't speak. She realised that the knot of unhappiness that had almost become part of her was melting, and a wave of joy and relief bubbled up inside her. She had Sam back. Surely nothing else mattered.

They sat holding hands, the tension between them gone, while Bono snuffled contentedly among the heaps of last year's leaves.

"Claire, I'm really sorry – "

"I've been so stupid – "

They both spoke at once, and stopped. Then they laughed together like they used to. Sam put his arm round Claire and she leaned against him, her body relaxed.

"Come back to my house," said Sam. "Dad's making pasta. And we can listen to some music."

"Sorry, Sam," she whispered, smiling at him, "I've got to go. Meet you here tomorrow?"

Claire ran home as fast as she could. She knew Michelle would have already left. The patio doors were open and she could see Mum in the garden, snipping daffodils to bring into the house.

Claire waved to her and dashed upstairs. Pulling on her new Levis and a denim jacket, she ran a brush through her hair. There was no time for anything else.

At the bottom of the stairs Mum was waiting for her, holding something in her hand. When she opened it, in her palm lay the silver earrings, fragile and gleaming.

Claire took them, kissed Mum's wet cheek, and stepped out into the sunlight.

About the Authors

MARY ARRIGAN was born in Newbridge and is a graduate of NCAD. She is the author and illustrator of the Mamó series of Irish language children's books. She has also written numerous English language books for the young, including *Andy, Zeph and the Flying Cottage, Dead Monks and Shady Deals, Landscape with Cracked Sheep* and, for teenage readers, *Searching for the Green, Saving the Dark Planet* and *The Dwellers Beneath* (White Ravens award). In 1991 she won *The Sunday Times*/CWA Literary award and, in 1993, the Hennessy award for Best Emerging Writer. She is a regular children's reviewer for *The Sunday Tribune*. She lives in Co Tipperary.

MARY BECKETT was born in Belfast and graduated from St Mary's Training College. She taught in Ardoyne for ten years. *Give Them Stones,* her adult novel, *A Belfast Woman* and *A Literary Woman,* her collections of short stories, are internationally acclaimed. Her children's books include *Orla Was Six, Orla At School, A Family Tree* and *Hannah or Pink Balloons,* which was the winner of a Bisto Merit award for 1995/96. She is married with five grown children and lives in Dublin.

MICHAEL CARROLL was born in Dublin in 1966 and has been called one of the "great new writers" of his generation. He is the author of *The Last Starship, Moonlight* and *She Fades Away.* His books and stories have won many international awards and have been translated into several languages. He lives in Dublin with his wife and two cats.

MARITA CONLON-McKENNA was born in Dublin. She is the author of the acclaimed award-winning famine trilogy, *Under the Hawthorn Tree, Wildflower Girl* and *Fields of Home.* Her other work includes the picture book *Little Star, The Blue Horse* (Bisto Book of the Year 1992/3), *No Goodbye* and *Safe Harbour* (shortlisted for the Bisto Book of the Year award 1995/96). She is married with four children and lives in Dublin.

JUNE CONSIDINE was born in Dublin and graduated from Holy Faith Convent, Finglas. She has written numerous books for children and young adults, including the highly successful Beachwood and Luvenders series as well as two books for teenagers, *View From A*

Blind Bridge (shortlisted for the Bisto Book of the Year award, 1992/93) and *The Glass Triangle*. She works as a journalist and editor. She is married with one son and two daughters and lives in Dublin.

MARGRIT CRUICKSHANK was born in Scotland and graduated from Aberdeen University. She is the author of the popular SKUNK series, as well as the picture book *Down By the Pond, Anna's Six Wishes* (Children's "Pick of the Year" Book Award, 1995), *Liza's Lamb* and *A Monster Called Charlie* (shortlisted for the RAI award, 1993). For teenagers she has written *Circling the Triangle* (winner of the RAI Special Merit award, 1993) and *The Door*. She has three children and lives in Co Dublin.

ROSE DOYLE was born in Dublin and graduated from TCD. She is a journalist whose work for young children includes *Tarantula!* and *The Invisible Monk*. For older readers she has written *Goodbye Summer, Goodbye* (winner of a Bisto Merit award, 1994/95). She also edited a *Christmas Treasury for Children,* an anthology of letters from Irish College 1935-1995, and has written a radio play and four adult novels. She has two teenage boys and lives and works in Dublin.

SOINBHE LALLY was born in Enniskillen, Co Fermanagh and graduated from Queen's University, Belfast. She has published numerous short stories, plays and satirical items with various newspapers and journals including *Irish Press* New Writing and *Atlantic Monthly*. She is the author of *Song of the River, A Hive For the Honey-Bee, The Hungry Wind* and *The Poolbeg Book of Irish Fairy Stories for Children* and is a recipient of the Hennessy Literary award. She is married with grown children and lives in Co Donegal.

CHRIS LYNCH was born in Boston to Irish-American parents. He is a graduate of Suffolk University, Boston, and holds an MA from the writing program at Emerson College. He is the author of several highly-acclaimed young adult novels including *Shadow Boxer, Slot Machine* and the Blue-Eyed Son trilogy, *Mick, Blood Relations* and *Dog Eat Dog*. He lives in Galway with his wife and two children.

SAM McBRATNEY was born in 1943 in the Lagan Valley, Northern Ireland, and studied at Friends' School Lisburn and at Trinity College Dublin (History). His first book was published in

1976 and there followed numerous books for the young, including the internationally acclaimed picture book *Guess How Much I Love You.* Among his other books are *Francis Fry, Private Eye, Art, You're Magic!* and *The Chieftain's Daughter.* McBratney's awards for writing include the Bisto Merit award (twice), the Silveren Griffel (Dutch) and the prestigious Abby (the American Booksellers' Book of the Year). He is married with three grown-up children.

GRETTA MULROONEY was born in London to parents from Cork and Offaly. She took a degree in English at the University of Ulster. She is the author of three children's books – *A Can of Worms, A Nest of Vipers, A Den of Thieves* – and one book for teenagers, *Crossing the Line.* Her first adult fiction, *Araby,* will be published by HarperCollins in 1998. She lives with her family in Northamptonshire.

JOAN O'NEILL was born in Dublin. She is the author of three best-selling books for teenagers: *Daisy Chain War* (winner of an RAI Merit award 1991), *Bread and Sugar, Daisy Chain Wedding* and two adult novels, *Promised* and *Leaving Home.* She is married with five children and lives in Co Wicklow.

SIOBHÁN PARKINSON was born in Dublin and is a graduate of Trinity College, Dublin. She won the Bisto Book award in 1996/97 with *Sisters No Way!* and has had two other books shortlisted for the award: *Amelia* (1993/94) and *All Shining in the Spring* (1995/96). Her other work includes *No Peace for Amelia, Off We Go – the Country Adventure, Off We Go – the Dublin Adventure* and *The Leprechaun Who Wished He Wasn't.* She is married to Roger Bennett, the woodturner, has one son, Matthew, and lives in Dublin.

TOM RICHARDS was born in Chicago. He is the author of *The Lost Scrolls of Newgrange, Hotfoot, Hotfoot 2: Lucky's Revenge* and *The Pirate's Den.* A screenwriter, his first film, *Merlin,* is currently in pre-production. He is married with three children and lives in Co Meath.

MARILYN TAYLOR is a graduate of University College, London. A school librarian, she is the author of three novels for teenagers: *Could This Be Love? I Wondered,* which received the International Youth Library's White Raven award, *Could I Love A Stranger?* and *Call Yourself A Friend?* She is married with three children and lives in Dublin.

155

About the Editor

Robert Dunbar is lecturer in charge of English at the Church of Ireland College of Education, Rathmines, Dublin. Additionally, he teaches a course in children's literature at Trinity College, Dublin, and organises and teaches on the Trinity College course leading to the award of the Diploma in Children's Literature. He is a regular reviewer of children's books for a wide range of newspapers, magazines and radio programmes. He served on three occasions as Chairperson of the Irish Children's Book Trust book awards committee and edited the first fifteen issues of *Children's Books in Ireland*.